FALLING

FALLING
DOUG WILHELM

FARRAR, STRAUS AND GIROUX · NEW YORK

44106

Copyright © 2007 by Doug Wilhelm
All rights reserved
Distributed in Canada by Douglas & McIntyre Ltd.
Printed in the United States of America
Designed by Irene Metaxatos
First edition, 2007
10 9 8 7 6 5 4 3 2 1

www.fsgkidsbooks.com

Library of Congress Cataloging-in-Publication Data
Wilhelm, Doug.
    Falling / Doug Wilhelm.— 1st ed.
        p.   cm.
    Summary: Fifteen-year-old Matt's life has been turned upside-down,
first when the brother he idolizes turns to drugs, then when a visit to a
chat room leads him to a classmate, Katie, whom he likes very much but
cannot trust with his family secret.
    ISBN-13: 978-0-374-32251-9
    ISBN-10: 0-374-32251-1
    [1. Self-actualization (Psychology)—Fiction.   2. Interpersonal
relations—Fiction.   3. Family problems—Fiction.   4. Basketball—
Fiction.   5. High schools—Fiction.   6. Schools—Fiction.   7. Drug
abuse—Fiction.   8. Vermont—Fiction.]   I. Title.

PZ7.W648145 Fal 2007
[Fic]—dc22

                                                        2006045293

FOR MARSHA
WITH LOVE

CONTENTS

FALLING

CHOICE

The first place he wasn't going to anymore, after school, was home. Instead he put on his headphones and he walked.

It was finally getting better to be out here walking. It was finally spring. Well, more or less. You didn't get much real spring in northern New England—you'd get a tease of a nice day, then next you'd get slammed with sleet, snow, freezing rain, or just plain rain. Or all of that. It was best not to have expectations. Just put your head down and deal with it. He had walked through all of it, every day after school, all winter long, no matter what the weather was.

And today wasn't bad. The air was softer, warmer at last. Standing on the steps in front of school, ignoring the kids joking and teasing each other and flowing out around him, he started to zip up his sweatshirt as usual, but then left it open. He felt the warm, soft air through his T-shirt. He walked down the steps and turned right, as he did every day after school, and he started to walk past the gym.

The gym was the other place he wasn't going into anymore, after school. It was in a high brick block that stuck out from the rest of the school, and around the corner on the Grove Street side it had narrow windows along the top of the wall. All through the winter, when he'd looked up there as he walked past in the afternoon, he had seen the yellow gym light and heard the guys or the coach yelling and the balls bouncing and the stop-and-start squeaking of their shoes.

He had known, all winter long, that if he'd ever pulled open the gym door and walked in there during basketball practice for the ninth-grade boys' team, it would have been a big thing. A major event. The guys would have all figured he'd finally come to his senses. Why, after all, would the kid who had been the best player on every school and AAU basketball team he'd ever joined, from fourth grade on, suddenly when he got to the freshman level—when he finally got the chance to put on the city uniform, just two steps from varsity—refuse to go out? Refuse to play, to practice, even to touch the ball? It didn't make sense. But he never explained, and he never pulled open the door. Never came close. Every afternoon, all winter, he had just walked by. Now the season was over and the bouncing and squeaking had stopped.

At the Grove Street light, he turned up the music in his headphones. The light was red and there were two crossing guards. Each day he had to decide which way to turn. This was his big choice of the afternoon: turn left and walk toward the little city's downtown, or turn right toward his own neighborhood and the house he wasn't going into—not till dinnertime, when the creeps and losers were gone.

He turned left and started to walk along Grove Street toward downtown. It was interesting, once you had left the school and the choices you'd made behind and you had the headphones on and the music turned up, and you were just walking and looking around. It was like watching a movie with a soundtrack—a film you could walk right through, but you weren't really part of. He wasn't in this movie anymore. He didn't want to be. So he just walked and looked around.

Cars swished past on the slightly wet street. In each, a face slipped by; you'd see it for a second and then it was gone. The sidewalk along Grove Street had been buckled here and there by the spring thaw, so that sections of it were tented up and others tilted down, like an obstacle course. He stepped off the sidewalk, onto the street, to go around the slow-walking guy in the old torn parka patched with duct tape. The guy in the patched parka always walked slowly, partly because of how he was, but also because he was looking for empty, tossed-away bottles and cans to redeem for the five-cent deposit. The man's head was bobbing around and a white plastic shopping bag drooped from his hand, with what looked like just a couple of empties inside. He had a lot of slow searching ahead before he'd have enough to take over to the redemption center. Along the street came a lady jogger in shiny purple tights, running with high steps and pushing a jogger's bicycle-wheeled baby carriage. In between the wheels was a kind of tent, of bright yellow nylon, with the baby zipped inside.

What was the point? The boy wondered this. He often did, walking and seeing the same sort of things day after day. What was the point of picking up empties for redemption, what was the point of jogging a baby inside a yellow tent? If a car were to suddenly swerve (maybe on a last patch of black ice) and kill him at this moment, would the world be any different? Not really. If the same thing were to happen to him in sixty years— let's say he still happened to be walking on Grove Street in sixty years—would it really matter then either? Was it supposed to matter? Did it ever?

He wasn't sure. Do lives *have* a point? All these people slipping by, these faces in the cars—do they need their lives to be something, to mean something, to leave more than a second's quick swish on a slightly wet street? Maybe they're all interchangeable faces in interchangeable cars, the way they seem to be right now: moving parts that just get tossed away after they're worn out or broken in an accident, and each part doesn't matter, not really. Maybe the whole machine is rusty and faded and creaky, like an old New England car after too many long winters.

He stepped off the sidewalk again, this time to walk around a man in a raincoat. But the man stepped aside, too. The boy stepped back on the sidewalk, but then so did the man. The boy looked up to see that the man was talking at him. He was a balding guy in a dark suit with a tan raincoat, and he was talking at him. He looked angry, or stern. The boy didn't get it. He switched off his music and took off the phones.

"It's a God-given talent," the man was saying. "When you have a talent like that, God wants you to use it. To *use* it. Why else would you have it, for God's sake?"

He just looked at the man.

Now the man pointed at him. "Who are you to tell God it was wasted—a wasted investment?" the man said. "Not to mention the other guys. You know what kind of season they had. They hardly won a game. It's just a shame. When a kid has something special and he just walks away from that special-ness . . ."

The man stepped back, looked at the boy, bunched his mouth up tight, and shook his head. He stepped past the boy and started walking. But as he did he said, loudly so the boy would hear: "It's just a goddamn shame."

CHAT

That evening in their apartment a block behind Grove Street, Katie Henoch and her mom finished their dinner and their after-dinner squabble, ending with their after-dinner slamming of doors. In her room now, Katie looked at the phone and the computer and decided, the phone first.

Tamra, almost always the first choice of her three best friends, answered, to Katie's relief.

"Hello?"

"Am I special enough?"

"Katie. Of course you are. Special enough for what?"

"For anything. For something. God, I don't know—that's just it. Am I special enough for *some*thing?" (Or someone, Katie thought, but didn't say.)

"You are very special. Exceptionally specially special," said Tam. "For example, you are the absolute queen of the unanswerable question."

Katie sputtered a laugh, spraying the phone. Then she felt grateful no one had seen her do that.

"But—please don't humor me," she said. "Everybody always humors me." By "everybody" she meant the brain trust: Tam, Sam, and Hope. For a long time, for the whole time since the four girls had started Jeffords Junior High School together in seventh grade, Katie's three best friends *had* been everybody to her. They had been through everything, all the changes, all the dramas of the middle-school years. They had got through it together. Now they were ninth-graders, and lately, though Katie never said this, even to herself, she didn't feel so totally complete with her best friends anymore. She didn't understand this feeling. She felt terrible for feeling it.

"We don't humor you, Katie," Tam said. "We love you. There's a difference."

"What's the difference between loving somebody and humoring somebody?"

Tam laughed. "There, you see? The queen."

"No, but seriously. Honestly. Why do people humor me? They don't humor you. We don't humor Sam or Hope."

"Sometimes we humor Sam."

"We don't. We tell her to snap out of it. That's not humoring her."

"So? Everybody's different. You're just you. We *like* you, Katie."

"I know. I do know. But . . . why?"

"Why what? Why do we like you?"

9

"Well, yeah. I mean no. I mean, why could somebody . . . you know . . . like me in a different way? You know?" Katie hunched over the phone, hoping to hear something she could gather in and hold.

"Well . . . you're the most loyal friend a person could have. Ever. There's nothing you wouldn't do. Second, you're smart as hell, and third, you're extremely nice-looking."

"Oh, *nice*-looking. God."

"What's wrong with that?"

"It's the kiss of death."

"It is not."

"It is too. It's like saying 'She has a really good personality.' "

"No it isn't, Katie, now stop!" Katie heard the sudden emotion in her best friend's voice. She felt terrible.

"I'm really sorry," she almost whispered. "I'm just . . . I'm not sure about a lot of things right now."

"I know. It's okay. You're okay."

"You think so?" Katie heard her own voice waver.

"Yeah—sure. I know so."

"Well . . . okay. Thanks. I better go."

"We can talk some more if you want to," Tam said.

"No, really, I better do homework. The police will be checking."

"Which, the mom police tonight or the teacher police tomorrow?"

"Does it matter?"

"Did you two get along tonight?"

"Of course not. She drives me crazy. Why can't parents

stay in some glassed-in area and just, like, slide you your food?"

"You're all she's got, Katie," Tamra said.

Now Katie was tearing up. "I better . . . go," she said. "I better do homework or something."

"Are you okay?"

"Yes. I think so. I'll call back later, okay? Or I'll IM. Will you be online?"

"I don't think so. I'm exhausted by instant messaging. As soon as I get on, like twenty people pop up and want to talk."

"That's 'cause you're people's hero, Tam."

"Phoo."

"You are."

"Oh phoo. Do your homework."

"Okay bye."

"Okay bye."

Katie hung up. It was true about Tam—she was the one girl, at least in their grade, who had achieved status and admiration without ever seeming to care at all about status and admiration. Nobody knew how she did that. Tam didn't know; if asked she would shrug. She was just totally herself. A whole lot of other girls wanted to be Tam, had wanted to be her at one time or another. But no one else could.

Katie had wanted to be Tam most of all, for the longest time. But Katie wasn't tall like Tam, she couldn't sing like Tam, she didn't effortlessly make straight A's like Tam, and she didn't have Tam's unusual relationship with boys, which centered on beating them at every game, every sport, every contest into which Tam could dare or taunt any boy into taking her on. Tam didn't always win, but she often did; she sure tried. This made her somewhat of a controversial character—not just with certain boys who didn't appreciate losing to a girl and had to bad-mouth her afterward, which then Tam didn't appreciate (there had been a couple of fights, which had not ended well for either side), but also with some girls who felt Tam was . . . what? Crossing the line, maybe. Or too full of herself. Or else she just made them uncomfortable, and they resented her for it. If Tam even noticed, she didn't care. This was another reason—her unconcern for what anyone else thought, at this self-conscious age—that those girls who didn't resent Tam, who weren't always running her down behind her back, tended to idolize her. If they couldn't be her, they wanted to be her best friend.

What those girls wanted, Katie had. She and Tam had been best friends for years. But lately Katie had almost begun to feel she was over Tam. This too made her feel horrible. She felt deeply disloyal—but it was true. Katie still loved Tam's escapades and her way of being so individualistic, but she wasn't infatuated with her anymore. Tam was still Tam. It was Katie who was changing.

Katie couldn't talk to anyone about this stuff. When you're feeling that you're not who you were and you're not sure who you are, and when that means you need something your best friends can't give you, you can't talk to your best friends about that, so who? Who could she talk to now?

Katie looked at the laptop on her desk, then at her backpack beside her on the bed with her homework inside. She went over to the desk, grabbed her laptop, and flopped back on the bed while pulling open the top. She woke the machine up with a tap on a key and took it online.

There was a place she'd been visiting lately, where she wanted to go again. She'd found it just messing around one day. She hadn't told Tam or anyone. Her friends were dead set against Katie visiting chat rooms, even youth-only rooms. Anyone could pretend to be anything, they said. But Katie felt okay about this room. It was on a site called justeens.com, a chat room called MeaningQuest. She'd just visited a couple of times so far, and had only listened, watching the conversations scroll along, wondering sometimes where the people were from. Were they even Americans? Sometimes she looked for clues.

Tonight, though, she wanted to talk.

KTbug: Is anybody there?
1wanderR: somebody
KTbug: Just somebody?
1wanderR: i guess. anybody else here?

1wanderR: i guess not
KTbug: But u r still somebody, right?
1wanderR: i could say no but . . . here I am
KTbug: U ever wonder if u are enough?
1wanderR: huh? no. i wonder what's the point
KTbug: Isn't it to find your destiny?
1wanderR: you really think there's destiny?
KTbug: Well . . . sure. I feel like I'm in a big play, and I'm
     standing offstage waiting to go on but nobody's told

me what my part is yet. I don't know how I'm
supposed to find out.

1wanderR: if it's a play what happens when it's over and
the curtain comes down?

KTbug: Don't know . . . We get to go home?

1wanderR: or maybe there's new actors tomorrow and
there is no home?

KTbug: Whoa! Can you please come in out of the void?

1wanderR: why?

KTbug: Isn't it cold out there?

1wanderR: yeah

KTbug: I bet

1wanderR: come in out of the void . . . that's not bad

KTbug: It just came to me

1wanderR: or at least put your voidcoat on

KTbug: Voidcoat? Is that like a raincoat?

1wanderR: whoa you are quick

KTbug: Hey be nice

1wanderR: be NICE? we're at the edge of the void and
you say be NICE?

KTbug: What better time?

1wanderR: oh right . . . that what mom would say?

KTbug: Mom would say, put your voidcoat on dear, I'm
empty

1wanderR: my mom would never say that. not improving
enough

KTbug: So u don't need a mom. That's good :)

1wanderR: i hate all smiley faces

KTbug: I can see why

1wanderR: so what IS the point?

KTbug: Goddess knows

1wanderR: whoa a goddess fancier . . . female no doubt

KTbug: Put your voidcoat on now dear

1wanderR: when do I get to take it off?

KTbug: Hey! this is a spiritual room. R u just some
    slimeball? If u r I'm signing off.

1wanderR: no don't go

KTbug: U r not really 50 & male & disgusting, right?

1wanderR: only male & disgusting

KTbug: Well sure. This is fun though. I mean kind of

1wanderR: kind of definitely

KTbug: Tell me about u? A little? Just so I know a little

1wanderR: 15 kind of out there, holes in voidcoat

KTbug: Patch voidcoat with black holes u know. More?

1wanderR: live in Vermont, of all nowhere places,
    depressing town. spend days confined to prisonlike
    setting called jeffords junior high

KTbug: What?

1wanderR: you never heard of it

KTbug: Sure, I mean no . . . What you do after school?

1wanderR: spend it walking streets of depressing town

KTbug: Uh . . . OK . . .

1wanderR: hey you are not a black widow, right?

KTbug: HUH?

1wanderR: you know—black widow. mates, then digests
    mate

KTbug: O. No. No digestion. Or mate. So far

1wanderR: what a relief. I mean about the digestion. the
mate too

1wanderR: still there? yo?

KTbug: Yes. If . . . someone were to see this wanderer . . .
what would someone see?

1wanderR: i dunno . . . hood up, headphones on. the
usual. why?

KTbug: Well . . . just imagining. Anything else u do? In
school or whatever?

1wanderR: no. used to but stopped

KTbug: Used to what?

1wanderR: played ball. but stopped

KTbug: Ball?

1wanderR: bball. basket

KTbug: Not too good? I can't make basket if dropped
thru while clutching ball

1wanderR: i was leading scorer last year—all last years.
but play no more right now

KTbug: No more? Uh . . . 9 grade?

1wanderR: yeah. howd you know?

KTbug: Well . . . You said 15. Lucky guess I guess

1wanderR: hey gotta go

KTbug: OK but . . . tomorrow night? Same time? 8?

1wanderR: if you wanna

KTbug: Sure . . . I mean why not? But on regular IM this
time, not public room. OK?

1wanderR: swear you are no black widow

KTbug: I swear. Wear your voidcoat till then OK?

1wanderR: sure bye

KTbug: 8 tomorrow OK bye :)

KTbug: Sorry about the face! R u there?

<1wanderR has signed off at 8:46 p.m.>

Katie signed off, too, feeling her heart thumping in her ears. She lunged across the bed and grabbed the phone.

"Tamra!"

"Katie?"

"Something just happened!"

"Did you get *any* work done?"

"No—Tamra! You will not believe who I was just in a chat room with!"

TRUST

To Katie it had just seemed amazing, to find herself alone in a possibly global chat room with a boy she recognized from her school—and a boy with whom she seemed to hit it off the way she did. What happened the next morning made her start to think this was more than just amazing.

Katie had never encountered Matt Shaw before. At all. They'd had no classes together at Jeffords. She knew who he was, but of course everyone knew who he was. He had been a rising star, and now he was a mystery. This morning she was thinking about him as she walked to school. It was a nice morning, with that fresh new sun-warmth of spring in the north that feels so different, almost feels surprising, because the weather has suddenly stopped being an enemy.

Some kids were clustered on the patio out in front of the main doors. Other kids sat or stood off to the side, looking sleepy or dazed or depressed, hugging their books. Katie threaded her way through. Her friends were not out here.

Just inside the main doors there was a short in-between space, then a set of metal-and-glass swinging doors that opened onto the main hall but were closed this morning. When Katie stepped into this inner space, there was Matt. He was standing by himself, looking at the wall. There was nothing on the wall, no posters or flyers or anything to look at. He was just standing there. Later, when the shock had worn off, Katie thought maybe he hadn't wanted to be outside with all those people, but he didn't want to be inside any more than anyone else.

In the moment, she froze. She heard the creaking and the click as the outside door swung shut behind her. Matt turned, and their eyes met. She hadn't known about his eyes. They were blue—not pale blue, like most blue eyes, but deeper. Unusually deep.

For a long second there was nobody else. Nobody. Then the bell rang, the outer doors blasted open, and the crowd spilled in around them, passing them. Matt turned away and slipped through the inner doors. Katie stood there as the last of the crowd washed past and left her, still standing there.

· • ● • ·

Immediately after school the brain trust met at Sam's house. Nobody remembered who had first called these four girls the brain trust—it might have even been a parent—but the name had stuck. It was an insider's term. The girls didn't refer to themselves that way outside their tight little circle, but inside it was accepted, often shortened to "the trust."

The trust had, of course, Katie: medium height and build, shoulder-length brown hair, shapely face, and warm, dancing brown eyes. It was hard to know who was brightest in this group, but Katie was definitely the most questioning. She was always questioning.

Then there was Tamra, tall, talented, and powerful, both in the trust and to the girls outside it. As for boys, most of them at this point were smart enough not to take Tam on in one-on-one basketball, or in anything else. She had played ball on the ninth-grade team and she was pretty good, but she wasn't passionate about that, maybe because the girls' team only played other girls. Anyway, she was Tam. She was the unspoken leader of the brain trust. She would pretend that wasn't so—her power, after all, was in not seeming to care about her power. But she was also used to things going her way.

Samantha, Sam, had the burden in life of being amazingly pretty. Before she'd blossomed she'd been a classic towheaded tomboy, always tearing around in jeans torn at the knees; now she clutched herself in constant fear that she would embarrass herself, that she would make a mistake, that she didn't look okay. She looked like a miracle. She had long, rich blond hair that any light seemed to want to keep on touching, plus a perfect body and blue eyes that she turned green with tinted contact lenses. Sam had the most friends of anyone in the trust—she would talk to anybody, possibly because she needed something from everybody, and she got perfect grades because she was petrified to get less. She tried so, so hard. Her parents were divorced and she was scared to go out with anyone for real, but she was obsessed with one particular guy, Darryl Casey, who was basically an idiot. He was effortlessly good-looking and he knew it. A number of girls were fixated on him. He had so far paid no special attention to Sam, but she was try-ing—that is, if you can try without having the self-confidence to actually do anything.

Then there was Hope. The rest of the trust loved Hope, though they couldn't necessarily say why. She was quiet, with long dark hair, and she was a little awkward, a little shy. She was pretty, though not in a way that anyone had much noticed yet because she wasn't classic popular pretty. Hope was a little punk in style, though not extreme, just mainly in the chunky boots and black-rimmed glasses she wore. She wrote and read a whole lot, and she always thought before she said anything—so when she did say something, the other girls tended to slow down and listen. Maybe that was what they loved about Hope. She tended to look at things a little more deeply, often with a sort of sly, sideways irony.

Hope had, for example, an imaginary relationship with the perfect guy. His name was Brad Giblet and he didn't exist, but every few days he had new characteristics. Hope would de-scribe Brad's latest profile with a sort of deadpan twinkle. Brad was the slightly satiric, definitely safe standard against whom all real boys looked pale and dorky and not that interesting.

So that was the trust. Among themselves the girls had al-ways been a little protective of Katie, a little awed by Tam, a little impatient with Sam, a little doting on Hope. Outside the group . . . well, for a long time there had hardly *been* any "outside the group." There had just been the trust.

Tam was the last to come into Sam's house and join the girls, who sat and sprawled on, and across from, the couch in the family room downstairs.

"Hey, what's up?" Tam said as she sank one hand deep into the bowl of popcorn.

"Definitely chillin'," said Sam.

"Oh yes," said Hope. "We are so cool."

"So who's Brad this week?" Tam asked her. "Who's Brad," not "How's Brad," was a running joke.

"Dark," said Hope. "Dark and moody."

"Oooh," said Katie.

"Moody and brooding," Hope said.

"Oooh," Katie said again.

"I thought he was a blond Nordic ski god," said Sam, looking puzzled.

"He was," Hope said.

Sam brightened. "Darryl looked at me in the lunchroom today," she said. "I was carrying my tray and he was with his boys but I *know* he looked up at me."

"Well of course," said Katie.

"He might have looked at you, but he never sees you," said Tam. "He's a pophead." "Pophead" was the trust's term for someone who, if you squeezed their head, you would hear a pop, because there was only air in there.

"Did I look okay?" Sam said, anxiously studying each face. "I mean, today?"

"You always look okay," said Tam. "Anybody who doesn't see you look okay is a pophead."

"No need to mention names," said Hope. "Like Darryl Casey or anything."

The girls giggled except for Sam, who said, "I wonder what he was thinking."

"As a pophead, he does not think," said Hope. "Except about himself."

"Be yourself, for God's sake, Sam," said Tam. "If somebody notices you, that's a real person."

Sam clutched herself. "Not everybody can be you, Tamra. I just need to, you know . . . spark his attention."

"Samantha, listen to me," Tam said, leaning closer. "You cannot be a flippit." (Flippits: girls who flip their hair when a boy goes by—girls who say things like "Ohmygod he's *all* I can think about." Girls like that were on a level, the trust believed, with the popheads and the twitters, who were girls obsessed with clothes, makeup, and, of course, boys. Flippits and twitters were similar, but twitters were more obvious and, to the trust, more pathetic.)

The girls had had their own male interests, once in a while—boys who were more actual than Brad Giblet and more accessible than Darryl Casey, yet for all four girls the ultimate priority, so far, had been each other.

"Darryl Casey has no spark," Hope said. "You could jump

out a window, land on him, and he'd just worry about his hair."

Tam shook her head. "However, meanwhile, hello," she said, "this is not the subject." She turned to Katie, who had felt, inside herself, like she was lunging at the bars of an invisible cage.

The others turned to Katie, too. Tam's eyebrows went up.

"Tell them," she said.

"I was in this chat room," said Katie.

"Katie, you're not supposed to go in chat rooms!" Sam said. "It's dangerous!"

"I know, but this was a *spiritual* room. For teens only."

Sam frowned. "Anybody can pretend to be anybody."

"But that's just it—nobody was in there at all, except for me and this one guy—and I could tell right away, just by the way he talked about stuff, that it was a guy about our age. You know how you can tell, right?"

The girls nodded. This was true.

"Then before long I realized who he was," Katie said. She watched this sink in, her heart double-thumping.

"Who?" said Hope.

Katie leaned over the bowl of popcorn. The others did, too. Drama was their life.

"Matt Shaw."

There were looks. "Matt *Shaw*?" said Hope.

"Yes," said Katie. She took a breath and let the name out again slowly, with the warm air. "Matt Shaw."

"The boy who wouldn't play?"

"Yes."

24

"He is . . . *so* hot," Sam said, wide-eyed.

"Samantha," Tam said warningly. "Do not push the twitter zone."

"Oh give it up, Tamra," she said. "You know he is."

"How do you know it was him?" asked Hope. "Did he say so?"

"Not exactly. But he said he's a ninth-grader in Vermont and then he said Jeffords Junior High, which naturally piqued my interest, since I could have been talking to someone in Argentina. So I asked about his interests, to see if I could get any clues to who he was, and he said he used to play basketball but he quit. I asked if that was because he wasn't good and he said he'd been top scorer every year till this year, when he stopped."

She paused. Tam said, "Narrowing the list of possibilities to one."

"Whoa," said Sam. "Matt *Shaw*. I mean, he is not just hot, he's . . . emblematic."

"He's *what*?" said Tam.

"Um . . . maybe that's not the right word."

"That would mean he's a symbol or something," Tam said. She looked at the others. "Is Matt Shaw a symbol?"

Katie blushed. Hope shook her head.

"Brad Giblet is a symbol," Hope said. "I should know. Matt Shaw is just a confused boy."

"What about?" Sam said. "What do you know?"

Hope shrugged. "Nothing factual. Just my impression."

"Maybe he's a symbol of *inner mystery*," Sam said, lighting up and looking eagerly at Katie, who looked eagerly back. "He has those blue, blue eyes."

"So do you, Sam," said Tam.

"Not like his. I wish I had eyes like his. But . . . what is that word for mysterious? That's what I meant. It sounds like emblematic."

"Enigmatic?" said Katie.

"That's it!"

Katie looked from face to face. "Is he unattainable? I mean, truthfully." She blushed again, but had to say it. "For me."

Tam said, "Calm down, Katie. You only talked in a chat room."

"I know, but we *really talked*. It was like we hit it off in this, I don't mean to sound pretentious, but this kind of cosmic way. We *were* talking about kind of cosmic stuff, actually—but we really connected. I know we did. It was almost like, I mean the way it happened, just him and me in the room, both being from here—what are the chances of that? It was almost like it was meant to happen."

She said this last in a lowered, unsure voice. Now she studied each friend's expression. Tam was looking pained.

"Katie," she said. "Nobody knows what's going on with this guy. He just *quit*. He wouldn't go out this year, and this was the *ninth-grade team*. It mattered, you know? And he wouldn't explain anything to anybody. Now he stays so totally apart. Nobody knows what's going on with him. At all."

"I hear he just walks around," Sam said. "After school. He's mysterious."

"He's *thinking*," Katie said. "About stuff. I happen to know that."

"It could be drugs," Sam said, and looked around for approval. "Well . . . it could be, right?"

"Oh come on," Katie said, her face suddenly hot. "Don't guess when you've got no clue, all right? Just because someone stops being what everybody else wants him to be doesn't make him . . . I don't know . . . a druggie or a dropout." She folded her arms indignantly.

"Okay," Tam said carefully. "But you *don't* know. I mean, you really don't. You don't know where he goes, or what he does."

"Or why," said Hope.

"We'll find out," said Sam, sitting up straight, all business now. "Okay. I'll ask everybody who knows anything. Tonight. You two can, too. We'll call, we'll IM. It'll be fun! He must talk to *somebody*."

"I know," Hope said. "He really has just one friend left— that kid who used to play in seventh grade, but then he was too short. That kid KJ. The one who wears the Michael Jordan stuff. I think they're neighbors."

"That kid is a poser," said Tam.

"Oh, he's just another confused boy," said Hope. "They're everywhere."

"Okay, so can you call him?" Sam asked. "Find out if Matt likes anybody, or if someone we know were to maybe like him, would he maybe . . ."

"No," said Katie.

"What?"

"No. None of that. Please."

Sam just blinked at her, like she didn't understand.

"Don't be hurt," Katie said. "Okay? It's just . . . This is different. For me, it is. I'm going to IM with him tonight. I don't want anything set up or stage-managed, I just want to *talk* with him. That's all." She sat back, way back, on the couch.

Tam nodded. "Good for you. Find out for yourself. Just be careful."

"He doesn't know who I am," Katie said from the couch's depths. "What could happen?"

"I have no idea," Tam said. "But there are things about him you don't know. Nobody knows."

"He's enigmatic," Sam advised.

"You're stepping into something without us," Hope said. "This is *so* un-Katie-like."

"Can't we just ask around?" asked Sam.

Katie popped back up. "If you do anything like that, I won't talk to you for a week," she said. "I'm *serious*."

Sam's tinted eyes widened. "Okay," she said. "Okay." All four of them sat there silently now, uncomfortable.

"Well," Hope said after a while. "At least he's no pophead."

"No," said Tam. "He's dark."

"And moody," Hope agreed. "And clearly brooding."

"Oooh," said Sam.

Katie said nothing. But she felt something surge inside.

CROSSOVER

Try and stop me," KJ said. "Just one time. Check?"

KJ bounced the ball to Matt. The custom in one on one is for the defender to accept that little pass, then give it back when he's ready to go. That's the check. But Matt didn't move, he just let the ball fall off his stomach. It *tap-tapped* on the driveway till KJ sighed, bent over, and picked it up.

After school, at the same time that the girls were meeting in Sam's basement, Matt had had to stop in at his house. He didn't want to, but the battery on his iPod had run down and he'd forgotten to charge it the night before. He'd had to plug it in and leave it all day in his bedroom. After school he had planned to run in, grab the machine, and then get out, but on the way to his house there was KJ, practicing in his driveway next door. KJ had begged Matt to come see the move he'd been working on. Matt had let himself be drawn over.

But now he just looked at KJ. He didn't bend into defensive position; but he was standing in the right place for a defender, so KJ started dribbling. KJ held out his right arm and pushed the ball downward to bounce it up a little high at his side, the way Michael Jordan would have. He leaned right and took a small step as if he were going that way. Matt didn't move. KJ's dribble bounded a little too high; he reached, cupped the ball, and shoved it back down on an inward angle. It bounced between him and Matt and came up the other side. KJ lurched after the ball, caught up to it, and with one shaky dribble and then a decent one he lifted it up and laid it off the backboard. Matt turned and watched.

The ball fell through. KJ caught it off the bounce.

"So?" he said. "Is that an MJ crossover or what?"

"It's better. Definitely. You've been practicing."

"Well yeah," KJ said, looking at his ball. "Still needs work though, huh?"

Matt shrugged and didn't answer. KJ bounce-passed the ball his way. Matt caught it without thinking, by habit.

"Show me," KJ said.

Matt didn't answer. Didn't move.

"For God's sake, Matt, I'm not asking for a *game*. Just show me, okay? One time. Show how MJ did it."

KJ was wearing a black Chicago Bulls road jersey with Jordan's number 23 in white and red, and very oversized North Carolina shorts in pale blue and white, which didn't go with the jersey in any way except that Michael Jordan had been both a Bull and a Tarheel. And he had on a pair of vintage-style Air Jordan shoes. Red and black, the original model, very possibly the ugliest basketball shoes ever made. KJ had paid, Matt knew, almost a hundred dollars for them, money he'd earned shoveling snow.

"I don't know how Michael Jordan did a crossover," Matt said. "Or if."

"So just show me a crossover. Come on."

KJ got between Matt and the basket and bent into the stance. KJ was dark-haired, on the short side, and squarish. Boxy. The two things he wanted most in the world, Matt knew, were both not going to happen. He couldn't watch Michael Jordan play a game in person, because of course Jordan had retired. For good this time. KJ knew this, of course, along with absolutely everything else about MJ.

The other thing KJ wanted, more even than that or anything else in his life, was to play—to wear the red-and-white uniform and play for the Raiders of Jeffords Junior High School, and then of Rutland High.

KJ didn't yet know for sure that this, too, would never happen. He practiced all the time—and even though he hadn't made the freshman team this past winter, or the eighth-grade team the year before that, he had hope. He often reminded Matt that MJ had been cut as a *tenth*-grader. KJ believed that if you wanted it bad enough and worked hard enough and believed in yourself, you could make it. But Matt knew that this dream of KJ's would also not be coming true.

He had never said this to his friend and he never would, but Matt knew KJ didn't have the size, he didn't have the quickness, he didn't have the agility . . . And whatever that special something is that a good basketball player needs, at the high-school level and above, KJ didn't have that either. If Matt could have given KJ all those things, just handed them over like a throwback jersey, he would have. For nothing. To KJ it would have meant everything.

Matt held the ball and looked at it. He could at least show him a move.

The dribble came feathery off his fingers. KJ bounced on the balls of his feet, ready and eager. Matt, tall and slender, was fluid as he took a half step to the right, dribbling while dipping his chin and shoulder that way, and KJ reacted, his weight shifting back; then the ball slipped between them going the other way and Matt's body went with it. Effortless dribble, long stride, soft layup. All one glide.

Matt turned back to KJ, letting the ball bounce and then start to roll down the long driveway. "Start to go right like you're really going, okay? When he reacts, you cross over."

KJ nodded. For a second he seemed just to stare at the driveway. Then he hurried after the ball, scuttling and then bending to scoop it up before it rolled away. He stood up straight and stayed there, cradling the ball in his arms, wearing his mismatched clothes, looking silently at nothing.

Matt came up to his friend.

"Kingsley James," he said.

"What," KJ said, not looking at him. "Don't call me that."

Matt nodded. He held out one hand, KJ stuck out his, and they did a shake. Then Matt pulled up his hood and started striding fast across the lawns toward his own house.

His parents were at work, as always in the afternoon. Neal, his older brother, was home, as usual in the afternoon these days. There was a car in the driveway that Matt had never seen before. That was typical, too. Sometimes they were decent cars, but usually they were pieces of crap like this one. It was a blue Chevy Cavalier, which was a crappy car to begin with, and now rust was eating away at the base of the body and creeping up from the wheel wells. The back window had a big American flag sticker that said "Support Our Troops."

Matt came through the empty garage, up the short steps, and in the metal door that led through a short hallway to the kitchen. From across the big kitchen he heard music, violent-sounding thrash music, pumping from Neal's room. Neal's room was off the far end of the kitchen, also facing the back patio and the backyard. It was like a separate apartment, which was a good thing: Neal had his own door to the patio, and Matt expected and hoped that the creeps and losers would go in and out that way, and would only use Neal's room—but here was this scrawny girl in a black T-shirt, foraging in Matt's family's kitchen.

Matt stopped. He stared at her. The scrawny girl had a pinched face and a torn-open bag of cookies in her hand. She had stuffed some cookies in her mouth, so many in fact that she was having a hard time chewing. She stood in front of the open cupboard where she had snatched the bag.

The scrawny girl leaned against the counter and looked him up and down.

"A young one," she said softly, and opened her eyes wide. "What you got for me, young one?" She said that like she was trying to be sexy or something, which was ridiculous and disgusting. Some crumbs were stuck to the corners of her mouth. Her long hair was stringy. Matt felt sick. Then he felt angry.

"Want some?" the girl said as she held out the ripped-open bag of Matt's family's cookies. She stepped toward him and put her other hand on her hip.

"Got some?" she said, trying to purr again. She stepped up much too close to him.

"I'll share," she murmured. "If you will."

Matt turned and stalked to Neal's door and pounded on it. The bass beat thumped against the door. The vocal screamed inside. No human answered Matt. He pounded harder.

"*What?*" That was Neal's voice, in there sounding annoyed.

Matt just kept pounding and pounding on the locked door. He pounded so hard, so angrily, that finally the door cracked open. Neal snarled, "What the *fuck?*"

Then Matt didn't know what to say. How could he say, "She's eating the cookies, Neal, our cookies! She's ruined the *cookies*, Neal!" How lame and stupid would that sound? So Matt just stood there, with the thrash music howling through the crack; then Neal twisted away and the door smacked shut in Matt's face. The lock clicked.

But the voice in Matt's head kept churning. *She shouldn't*

BE *here, Neal! She's in our kitchen! She's ruined our cookies! Don't you remember ANYthing, Neal?*

Matt turned away from the door. The girl had her whole fist in the bag now. She was chewing with her mouth open; he could see cookie mess in there. Crumbs on her T-shirt. Worse than disgusting. She put the ravaged bag down on the counter and stepped toward Matt again. Her expression was different now. More like pleading.

"*Share,*" she said. "Come on. Share." She stepped too close again. "I would," she whispered. "You know I would."

Matt faked going left, and she moved that way; he slipped to the right, past her, and darted up the stairs.

In his room he swung his heavy backpack onto the bed, then unplugged the iPod that was sitting on his dresser. He shoved the little unit into one pocket of his sweatshirt and, more carefully, slipped the folded headphones in the other pocket. Stepping back into the hall, he pulled his bedroom door closed behind him. Then he reopened it, reached around and pushed the lock button. Before closing the door he stretched his arm up to feel the key on the top of the door frame. He thought a second, then plucked the key off and slid it into his pocket. First time he'd done that. He shut the door and slipped fast down the front steps, then out the front door. He headed quickly down the long driveway.

· ● ·

In Matt's neighborhood the new green leaves were just unfurling on the trees. They made Grove Street, as he walked along it, seem leafy and sheltering. The cars whizzed by too fast, rushing out of town. The houses out here were all nice, the lawns manicured; then you came to the country club, with its deep-green golf course undulating along the left side of the road. Matt, walking away from town, pulled on his headphones and pulled up his hood. He selected a song and turned up the sound. Against a big beat, Tupac Shakur started saying it was just him against the world.

Matt loved a certain type of deep-city hip-hop, a certain type of song. He had pulled the stuff he liked off audio sites and CDs till his player was a solid little cabinet of the ones that fit him, that spoke to him. The iPod was his one and only companion. He trusted it like a friend. It held his music.

Out here it was raining very softly now, like a mist in the air. The bright and delicate new green of spring was everywhere, freshly growing on the trees and the lawns, sometimes mingled with the dark green of pine trees. Matt did notice the new green, and he knew it wouldn't last. Nothing lasted. As he came past the golf course, the rain started thickening. A few players hurried off the course to the clubhouse in white carts, and in the parking lot a few others were stowing clubs in the trunks of their nice cars. Out on the road, Matt walked by the golf people unseen, as if he and they were creatures in a divided universe. He kept on walking.

Sometimes Matt felt like something good might be near, like something good might happen soon. He had no idea what, but sometimes he could feel it in his chest, a sneaky feeling that was exciting and kept him looking around as he walked. As far as he knew, this feeling had no basis. Nothing good had happened at all. He didn't like to think about Neal anymore, and generally he was able not to—but now in his mind he saw the scaggy girl with the cookie mess in her open mouth, and he felt smacked again with anger and hurt. Why did she have to eat the *cookies*? And right then, without wanting to at all, he could almost smell the other cookies—the real cookies, when he and Neal would take them from the oven after games.

They always made chocolate chip. Their mom would buy batches of those easy-bake tubes of dough, and leave them in the fridge. The brothers would split open a tube, line up spoonfuls of dough on greased cookie sheets and slide them into the oven. They were good at this, they did it right. While the cookies baked, they would talk.

They talked about everything—everything they cared about. Girls, to some degree. Matt wasn't yet interested in this subject in a personal way, but he admired and appreciated Neal's adventures. As a basketball star in a sports-minded town, Neal had a lot of admirers. He took them for granted. But when Neal noticed Stephanie, that was different. Matt knew it even before Neal did. He had a sneaky feeling in his chest about this girl, just from the way Neal casually mentioned her.

"Yeah . . . she's pretty okay," Neal said, and then he smiled in a very private way, like there might be more but he was keeping it to himself for now. "She doesn't come to the games though. Not yet, she doesn't." And then he looked at Matt and smiled more broadly, because they both understood she'd be coming soon.

Mainly they talked about basketball. As they waited for their cookies they'd start to break down Neal's most recent game. Their mom would be gone again, off to some evening meeting or whatever, their dad off somewhere, too. They'd be taking a homework break and they would talk about the game.

Matt was a sharp observer. Neal would listen when his little brother said he'd forced up a shot on a baseline drive in the third quarter, when he'd beaten his man and another defender had dropped down to cover, leaving Neal's teammate open under the basket. "Oh," Neal would say, grinning, "and I suppose *you* would have passed it, Mister Unselfish?" But Matt knew he liked the criticism. It helped him get better. Neal was always working to get better; that was how Matt had learned to do it, too.

Past the golf course now, it was like walking in a green tunnel. The sky was gray and lowering, the rain denser. On the roadside the rain had drawn out the slugs. They were orange and new, not big and fat yet. Matt stomped on each one he saw. Each time he flattened a slug it let his anger out just a little. Sometimes what he thought at first was a slug was a cigarette butt, the orange filter end. That made him mad all over again. He kept walking, looking for the little orange slimers, the real living ones, to squash.

Neal had come to Matt's games, too. Whenever he could. Generally he was the only one in the family who could come— most sixth-, seventh-, and eighth-grade games were after school, and their parents were working then or else busy with their clubs and committees and fund-raisers or whatever. Later, in the kitchen, the cookies would come out of the oven, and they smelled and tasted warm and rich as Neal would talk about the things Matt had done well. He would have seen and remembered not just the moves and buckets but the passes, the assists, and the defense, the times when Matt made his teammates better. You could tease Neal about how he was the Raiders' varsity hotshot, but he had good hoop values. Those values went together, in Matt's memory, with the rich warm smell of their cookies.

Matt was wet now and hot under the sweatshirt, which was starting to soak through. He could feel the steamy moisture on his back, and suddenly he worried about his iPod in the front pocket with the cord coming up to his headphones. What if the machine got wet—would it short-circuit or something? He couldn't lose his music. He turned quickly and headed back toward home. Walking huddled over his pocketed player to shelter it from the now-enveloping rain, Matt hurried up his front walk, came quickly in the front door, and slipped up the stairs. He let himself into his room, then locked himself in. He stripped off his clothes, carefully dried the iPod, laid it on his desk, pulled on a dry T-shirt and shorts, and sat on his bed in the gloom. For a while he just sat there.

In Matt's memory those good afternoons were all baked together, warm and rich like the cookies in a way. When everything started going bad—he remembered that in a more jerky, awkward way, like an antique silent movie whose action never really seemed real. Neal's Raider career had ended last March with a semifinal playoff loss, even though Neal scored thirty-seven points. Matt played AAU ball in the spring as always, and Neal came to a couple of his games, but he was a senior, he had other stuff going on. Matt started to have that feeling of something ending, slipping away—but at first it was in the way that he knew was normal. Neal would go to college. He would play ball. If it wasn't too far away, Matt would go watch.

But Neal wasn't offered any scholarships. He'd wanted to play Division I ball, had counted on that, maybe too confidently—but Vermont ballplayers rarely get noticed by Division I schools, and Neal didn't get any offers. He was only six foot three. In high school he'd been a shifty, slippery forward who could get to the basket from anywhere; on a top college team at that height he'd have to be a point guard or a shooting guard, and he wasn't speedy or slick enough for that. He'd set his sights too high, Matt knew it. But Neal was stubborn. He'd always been the star, the number-one player, and he couldn't adjust. Didn't want to. He could have played at any small college, maybe at a Division II university. A scholarship wasn't essential either, their parents had money. But Neal got stuck inside himself. He'd told everyone he would play DI, and when no big-time coach came to sweep him away, he just dug in. Wouldn't listen to his friends, or even Stephanie. Matt watched the rest unfold in that jerky, semi-real way.

Steph did get a scholarship, and she went off to play flute and field hockey at the University of Vermont. That dug Neal in deeper. Last summer had been strange. Neal and Matt hardly talked at all. Matt worried. All of Neal's real friends left, all his motivated friends. They went to college. Neal was locked in now, stuck with his choice that hadn't worked. It was sad. For a while, in the fall, he hardly left his room. Then he started to have new friends. Loser friends.

Matt heard a flat, smacking sound outside, then again. KJ was practicing. Matt glanced out: there was the squarish figure in the driveway next door, doing his crossover move again and again in the softly falling rain.

Why exactly Matt had refused to go out for the freshman team last fall, his first chance at last to wear the real Raider uniform—why he wouldn't even touch the ball—was something he couldn't explain, hadn't totally thought through. Boys don't always. Sometimes they just do stuff. Matt talked about this with no one. People tried: the coach, his old teammates, KJ, even his parents. Matt just turned them away.

Neal never asked. He didn't seem to notice. Neal was a different person now. Once in a while he'd be nice, happy, though in a very loose and different way; but mostly he treated Matt like crap. He didn't acknowledge anyone in the family anymore, just gave you a cold look that said to stay out of his way, out of his room. Out of his life. If you crossed any of those lines he'd push you back over with cold brutal words. The jerky movie played on.

People Matt had never known before would come over in the daytime and hang around. Most of them Matt never saw, because he didn't want to. He wanted nothing to do with what he knew was going on at his house in the daytime, so he stayed away. The losers and their cars would be gone at the end of the day when his parents came home, usually briefly before going out again. After his parents got home was when Matt would come home, too.

If the subject came up, Matt's parents would say Neal was "taking some time off." They said he was "finding himself." His parents were so used to the boys bringing praise and applause to the family, as they were always doing, too, that they didn't appear to be giving this a second thought. It was just a pause in the applause. But Matt knew Neal wasn't finding himself.

At last Matt heard a familiar-sounding car come up the driveway. His mom was home. He turned on the lamp by his bed and unlocked his door. But he stayed in his room.

CLICK

She'd had to get away from her friends. After she fled Sam's house that afternoon, Katie could only think about this guy. Thoughts and questions and feelings whizzed through her on crisscrossing orbits in bewildering ways. What would he be doing right now? He had incredible eyes. Did he like anyone? Eight tonight. Would he remember? What did he like to eat? What did he listen to? Had he noticed her this morning? Why did he walk, *really*, why? And where did he go?

Lately she'd been wondering about destiny. She'd been feeling she had no idea what hers was. Could he be her destiny? But can another person be your destiny? Isn't it more about who you are? Who was she? What was she made for? Did *he* think about stuff like this? When he was walking, what did he think about? And was this all she was ever going to be, this oddly unformed protoplasmic entity who didn't quite fit with her best friends anymore and had these feelings and weird questions pinging around inside her like a . . . like a . . . like what?

She didn't know. She couldn't even think of a *metaphor*.

She wanted to know him.

She didn't think he liked anyone, at least not anyone in school. Word would have gone around if he did. But about the rest, she really didn't know. She had to admit this was a little strange, that she would feel she so much liked someone she really didn't know anything about—and he was such a well-known person, yet people knew so little about him. Why did he quit playing? That's what everyone had asked, back in early winter when it was the talk of the school. But why really? And what did he do instead? Was it dangerous? Was he dangerous? And couldn't she maybe use a little danger in her life?

Katie, she thought. *Are you crazy or dumb or just hopelessly naive?*

But he wasn't *really* dangerous. She knew that. Somehow she knew him. She didn't know how, but somehow she knew that she knew him.

She tried to focus on details. What did she know? Well, his eyes . . . but no. Too much. Something else. His sweatshirt. She'd noticed his sweatshirt that morning. It was gray. Dark gray, and it had the dark red silhouette of a hand grenade on it. No words, just that. This was the only other detail she could remember, and it launched her into a new eruption of questions: Why a hand grenade? Hadn't she seen other boys wearing shirts with that on them? Maybe. She wasn't sure. Did this mean he was dangerous? Oh no; back to that. Well . . . was he angry about something? She'd seen enough preposterous tough-guy-against-the-world movies on Friday nights to know how hand grenades worked. If you pulled Matt's pin out, would he explode?

Katie, she thought, *it's just a sweatshirt*. Yes, but . . . was he in trouble? Was the sweatshirt a cry for help? *Katie, for God's sake—it's a sweatshirt.*

All she wanted was to know something. To know one thing about him for real. To know one thing about herself for real. To know something about the two of them. If there could be a "them." An *us*. She had never wondered about an *us* before, not really. Not a boy-girl *us*. Now the three hours and ten minutes until eight, till they would talk, *if* he remembered, seemed an impossibly long-stretching desert of dry and empty time. She didn't know what to do. She'd have to go home, get through . . . oh God, dinner with her mom . . .

· · ● · ·

KTbug: R u there?

KTbug: Hello?
1wanderR: yo. sorry
KTbug: I was worried!
1wanderR: sorry really
KTbug: Everything OK?
1wanderR: sure parents just leaving
KTbug: On Wed. night? Where 2?

1wanderR: oh who knows. meetings, leagues, work late . . . always something. wassup tonight?

KTbug: Not much. Usual battle with maternal overseer parent. U got 2?

1wanderR: 2 what?

KTbug: Parents.

1wanderR: yeah I think. you?

KTbug: Just maternal overseer.

1wanderR: where's your dad?

KTbug: Who knows. Gulf War vet, went wacko, gone.

1wanderR: sorry I shouldn't have asked

KTbug: No it's OK.

1wanderR: it is? why?

KTbug: Just used 2 it.

1wanderR: so you live where?

KTbug: O, u know . . . nowhere special really.

1wanderR: sounds like my town

KTbug: Sure . . . they're all alike, right?

1wanderR: are they?

KTbug: Dunno. So you have bros or sister?

1wanderR: 1 brother

KTbug: Older? Younger?

1wanderR: older

KTbug: U get along?

1wanderR: used to. you got any?

KTbug: Just me and my mom.

1wanderR: you get along?

KTbug: Used to.

1wanderR: how old are you anyway?

KTbug: Same as u.

1wanderR: oh you remember?

KTbug: Sure—u r 15 like me. What do u like to do most?

1wanderR: most?

KTbug: Yes. Be clean now :)

1wanderR: hey no smiley faces

KTbug: O sorry! I forgot. But what?

1wanderR: dunno. i walk a lot. you know? listen to jai
    quest. 2pac

KTbug: Favorites?

1wanderR: yeah

KTbug: Deep. Wear your voidcoat?

1wanderR: thought you had that

KTbug: I would like to have it. I would give it to u.

1wanderR: you would?

KTbug: Yes I feel sad 4 u

1wanderR: you do? why?

KTbug: U just walk, and u need voidcoat. U have friends?
    U like anyone?

1wanderR: not so much. most people are "disappointed"
    in me

KTbug: They are? Y?

1wanderR: i stopped doing what they expect. ever try it?

KTbug: Nothing I do that everyone expects. Except ask
    questions.

1wanderR: so I notice

KTbug: It's 2 much?

1wanderR: no. i like it. most people's questions i don't
     like. yours are different tho
KTbug: Am blushing now.
1wanderR: wish I could see that
KTbug: Whoa . . . so . . . so u don't like anyone?
1wanderR: i don't trust anyone

Katie stopped. She stared at the screen. Shook her head,
and took a deep breath.

KTbug: U need to trust somebody.
1wanderR: no one around. but thanks
KTbug: U believe in fate?
1wanderR: is this a black widow question again?
KTbug: No! Not poisonous. Honest. Do u?
1wanderR: what you mean fate?
KTbug: Like in destiny. As in can you meet the person
     destined 4 u
1wanderR: no I don't. you really believe that crap?
KTbug: Why not? :(Ooops, sorry again . . . How do u
     know there's not the one right person 4 u? Maybe u
     already met and u don't know.
1wanderR: i don't think so
KTbug: Why not?
1wanderR: like i told you i live in emptyville usa
KTbug: Isn't that perception? Is it mt cause you see it that
     way?
1wanderR: mt! i like that

KTbug: Thanks. So what do u believe? Really?

1wanderR: i m mt r u 2?

KTbug: Please—be serious.

1wanderR: i m

KTbug: That's who u r—just mt inside?

1wanderR: ok no. i m a warrior. only have what's inside

KTbug: Huh? Say more.

1wanderR: like jai quest says . . . life is war to survive. like
2pac says . . . no allies just me against the world. i get
strength i need from the songs & from inside

KTbug: But that's so sad!! Y no allies??

1wanderR: hey, trust no 1, no 1 can kill you

KTbug: u r only 15 and u say that? YYY?

1wanderR: simple. someone u trust someone u tell all to
can sell his soul to the devil. just like that

KTbug: U know that?

1wanderR: sure do

KTbug: O Matt that is so sad!!!

1wanderR: what?

KTbug: I m :'(4 u . . . O! sorry about face! again!

1wanderR: how do you know my name?

KTbug: What?

1wanderR: how you know my name?

KTbug: O no

1wanderR: you lied to me

KTbug: No! I didn't lie!

1wanderR: you're spying on me

KTbug: No! I'm not!

1wanderR: bye
KTbug: NO WAIT!!!

<1wanderR has signed off at 8:32 p.m.>

Katie stared, breathing hard and raggedly, at the screen. Nothing more. It was as if she had heard the click out loud when he signed off. He was gone.

IN MY ROOM

Katie neither IM'd nor called anybody else that night. Not Samantha, not Hope, not even Tam. Normally she and they would have scrutinized and analyzed every gesture, expression, grunted word, or other scrap of communication that one of the girls had received from a boy who was of new interest. There had been several boys of interest for Sam, of course, and a few for Katie and for Hope. Even one or two brave souls had liked Tamra, usually until they'd had their noses rubbed into a loss in one on one, Ping-Pong, rock-scissors-paper, hangman, or any other competition Tam could lure, challenge, or taunt them into.

But this boy was different. So Katie didn't hop online or grab the phone. Instead she sat there on her bed and looked out the window.

She and her mom lived in a two-bedroom apartment in the section of tired-looking houses just below Grove Street, close to the school and downtown. At night there was almost always something happening out there. Tonight, now that the rain had stopped, across the street an older teenage girl was outside holding a baby wrapped up in a blanket. The end of the blanket was trailing down and the girl was arguing hard with a tall guy who was trying to get in his car.

The girl stood on the bare wood steps of her little apartment building, outlined by the light of a yellow bulb in the hallway behind her. She clutched her baby and yelled at the boy; he bent into his car, slammed his door, and rolled up his window, and then she was shrieking at the glass. He backed angrily out the driveway. The car swung onto the street, then it shot forward and away as the girl stalked to the end of the driveway to yell at its taillights. When the girl walked back into her house, the baby's blanket was unraveling farther and the girl looked, even from up here, like she was shaking.

Katie knew she hadn't asked Matt the right question. That was it, wasn't it? Of course she knew what had happened, that she'd used his real name, but that was almost too horrible to think about—that she had made such a mistake and blown it so totally—and now what was she going to do? So instead she wondered about the question she hadn't asked. What was it?

Katie was a question-asker and tonight she knew, she really knew, that if she had only asked Matt that one magic question, he would have loved her. *And* he would have been free. He wouldn't hurt so much anymore, and he wouldn't be so captured by whatever it was. Whatever it was, it wouldn't let him be a kid anymore at all—and it wouldn't let him play basketball and be a hero, starring on the freshman team that was supposed to be the pride of Jeffords Junior High. If Katie had only known what to ask, she knew she could have freed him to be that hero again. To be himself again. Maybe to like somebody who really, really liked him. If only she'd asked him that exact question . . . or known what that question was.

It was like that girl out there. The girl was now standing on her bare steps smoking a cigarette, still holding the baby in its half-unraveled blanket. Katie knew that girl just hadn't said the right thing to that guy, or asked him the right thing. Guys need . . . well, what do they need? Katie wasn't sure—she had no dad, and little real experience—but she knew they needed to do whatever they had to do. It was in them, to be that way. If you wanted them to love you, you had to show them you believed they could do whatever it was they needed to do, and not be shrieking and trying to pull them back, to hold them back. If you did that they'd burn rubber getting away. Like that guy.

Wasn't that right?

But she hadn't shown Matt. She hadn't freed him. Instead, oh God, her fingers had typed his real name; and now, along with whoever else had betrayed him (what had he said, sold their soul to the devil?), now he thought she had, too. Oh God. He thought she had lied to him, spied on him, somehow set him up. Oh God, it was too much to even think about.

What could she do?

She looked at her fingers. They did this. They had typed his real name. If she could have chopped off her fingers, just to have that moment back, would she do it? Well, maybe one finger. Two? What about two on each hand? Would she go that far? She might. She wasn't sure. She felt like she'd do anything. But would she?

Then it hit her. The question. It was simple!

Why?

Katie had been asking *Why?* all her life, so often that it had sometimes driven people a little bit crazy—her mom, an occasional beloved teacher, the brain trust. Yet she hadn't thought to ask it of Matt.

Why don't you play? Why do you just walk and listen to your music? Why won't you tell anyone why? Matt, what's going on?

Wait. *That* was it. Had anyone just asked Matt what was going on in his life? Yes, everyone asked why he didn't play basketball—because everyone wanted him to play, right? Sure. But nobody, she suddenly knew, nobody had just asked what was happening that had changed him like this. Maybe it had nothing to do with basketball, but it had to be something. People don't just change like that, act like that, cut themselves off like that, for nothing.

Sitting up on her bed, staring out the window, seeing nothing—the girl had finished her cigarette and taken her baby back inside—Katie knew that was the question no one had asked. Maybe if someone—a person who truly cared about him—asked him that, then whatever had cut him off could unlock him and let him go.

She knew it. She *had* it. And she had blown her chance to ask it.

In fact, just like that guy in the car, who she knew was the baby's dad and didn't want to deal with it, Katie knew Matt had stormed away because he thought she didn't care about him. He thought she only wanted something from him, like everyone else did. She had blown her chance to show him this was different. She was different.

For a long time now, more and more, Katie had been wondering who she was, who she *really* was, and what there was for her to do. Now she knew. She was the girl who cared, who truly cared, about this boy. She was the one who could set him free. But first she had to find her way to the place where he would know that he could trust her, and then she could ask him the question and understand the answer, and that would make everything okay. And he would know, then, who she really was, too.

That was it. That was it. That was why she was here. That was all that really mattered.

Wasn't it?

· · ● · ·

At night in his part of Grove Street, where the houses were large and the driveways long, nothing much ever happened outside Matt's house. Unless KJ was working on moves and shooting in his driveway, there wasn't much to see out there.

In here, Matt pulled on the headphones and turned on the iPod. Its little window came alight, a bright rectangle with a list of artists and songs. He paged down to Jai Quest.

Jai Quest was who he mainly listened to, these days. That's

because Jai Quest knew. Matt chose "Got to Go." He sat back on his bed and listened. The beat came on, spare and strong, then the lyric.

> *I got to go*
> *Got to go*
> *Got to find it*
> *Find my flow*
> *Got to go*
> *Got to go*
> *Got to find it*
> *Find my flow*
>
> *Don't know how it happened, but I*
> *Can't find the flow*
> *Get any high or weapon but you*
> *Can't buy the flow*
> *All them suckas they don' know*
> *Shit they didn' neva know*
> *'Bout the flow the real flow*
> *But I know*
> *Yeah I do*
> *Yeah I did*
> *Yeah I did know yeah*
>
> *Got to find it where it's hid*
> *Got to get it like I did*
> *On the mic*

You don' know
Understand it got to go
Got to get it
They don' know
Go alone
That I know
Can't explain it but I got to
Yeah I got to
Got to go
Got to go
But I'm comin back tho

Yeah I'm comin back yo
Yeah I swear it, got to know
Comin' home when I find it
When I get it, back to you
Got to know, baby please know
Baby you just got to know

Got to find it
Time to go
Got to find it
Find my flow
Go alone
That I know
Got to go
Got to know
Yeah, you just got to know

Got to know
Got to know
Yeah
Somebody got to know

Sometimes he missed it really bad. It wasn't people watching, the clapping and cheering, you didn't really hear that half the time anyway—and that stuff was fine, it was good, and so was people treating him like he was someone special. Sometimes he had wondered who they thought he was anyway. Other times he'd thought, yeah they were right, he *was* special, but he didn't really know about that. In every other way he was pretty normal. He was bright enough but he didn't do that great in school, and he was awkward with girls. He got shy and didn't know what to say to them, or to people who told him he was great. But he could *play*. And he knew it. He missed the guys, sure, and he missed the games—but what he really missed was what he could not feel anymore.

The flow. Yeah. Knowing you could step on the court and make it happen. You practiced, sure. But then, when you walked out there, you could just go. You could flow, that was it: you created and you didn't totally know how. You just knew you could, so you did. It wasn't thinking and it wasn't imitating somebody else's moves, though you always looked carefully when you watched good players play. But when you played . . . it was something you couldn't explain. Neal used to know. It didn't come from thinking about it.

And the song was right—it wasn't there anymore. Matt had

felt all year like he just couldn't step on the court. He couldn't. Instead he had to go, like the song said, the only way he could. He had to walk and walk, search and search, not knowing what he was looking for. He also understood, without thinking about this either, that after Neal gave up on it, after Neal gave up on himself, Matt couldn't play the game anymore. Not while his brother was like this. There were some things more important than basketball. Some things he couldn't do anything about. So he walked, he listened to his songs, and he looked around, hoping for something without knowing what.

Matt understood full well, without knowing all the details or really wanting to, why home after school was the place where he did not want to be. He wasn't stupid. He had a pretty good idea what was going on in the daytime when his parents weren't home. He'd seen the loser friends, if they were friends at all, coming in and out, leaking into the kitchen sometimes like that girl. They would look at you with scary cold or sneaky scheming eyes; or they would be arguing harshly or whining at each other about sharing stuff. Matt wasn't sure what the stuff was exactly, but basically he knew. They brought it here, they did it here. They hung around. His house was a place to be wasted.

His brother acted like he had no feelings anymore, and like he didn't give a crap if Matt had any. When they did cross paths, in the kitchen sometimes, Matt was just a thing in Neal's way. Along with being mean and snappy now, Neal also looked more and more like the losers. He was skinnier and pimply. His eyes were sometimes soft and vague, sometimes scary and urgent, but usually flat, like nothing was back there at all.

Matt did sometimes wish there was someone he could talk to . . . but there was no one you could trust. No one. He couldn't tell anyone anything. If anybody found out, if what was happening in his house got out in any way, it would disgrace his family, maybe destroy it. His parents' whole world of positive image and public involvement, and of admirable sons you could be a little smug to everybody about, would fall apart. He didn't think they could handle it—and that would only be the start. His brother might go to prison, if he didn't die. Matt understood that the losers and his brother were not just smoking weed in his house. The whole thing was much more serious than that, and someone was going to find out. Something was going to happen. All Matt could do was stay away, knowing it could all come crashing in at any time.

So he couldn't trust anyone. Or talk to anyone. Even that stupid girl on the Internet—he'd thought for half a day that maybe she was okay, maybe she was different, but then he realized she had done a search on him or some such thing. People could do that now. It was ridiculous. You couldn't trust anybody at all.

In the raw trueness of his music he felt . . . like he needed to feel. Like a warrior, out there far from home in a lonely, empty, secret war that he could never win. He knew he couldn't. *It's just me against the world.* So he took refuge in the rhythm; he walked with the rhythm; he sat now with his head going and the rhythm working in him, and the rhythm gave him something like the feeling of the flow. When he turned the iPod off, it faded—it wasn't inside him to rely on, like it had been be-fore—but he could turn it on again and there it would be.

At least the rhythm would be there. Every day after school, and every night like tonight in his room, the rhythm and the raw, true rhyming would make it feel, for a little while, more or less okay.

PURPLE
ICE CREAM

The next day at lunch, the brain trust descended on her. Tam wanted to know. They all wanted to know.

"Well?" said Sam, setting her tray down so fast that everything on it rattled and made Katie want to shriek. Katie didn't say anything. She saw the other three girls look quickly at each other as they all sat.

"Katie," said Tamra, "did you talk to him?"

Katie nodded and looked at her food. The girls traded glances more openly now.

"He was a jackass, wasn't he," said Tam. She leaned back, folding her arms. "I was so hoping he wouldn't be a jackass."

"He's not," Katie said, suddenly passionate. "It wasn't like that. At all."

"Well, what's he like?" asked Sam, her eyes alight. "Are you going out? Are you talking again?"

Katie looked from one friend's face to the next. Tamra was tight-lipped and skeptical, Sam looked annoyingly eager, and

Hope's eyes were soft and sympathetic. Katie felt crowded and badgered.

"I just . . . I can't talk about it, okay? Nothing much happened. Well, something happened, but I can't talk about it."

"Why not?" said Sam. "Does he like you?"

"Does he like you," Katie repeated in a soft, parroting voice. "Does anybody ever think what a childish question that is?"

Now they looked shocked. Sam's eyes were wide. But Katie couldn't stop.

"I mean, what if it's not about everything people always think it's about? What if it's not about stupid phone calls and teenage romance and movie dates, and having four or five IM conversations at the same dumb time and wearing someone's game jersey? What if it's not about *any* of that?"

She stood up. Tam and Hope just stared. Samantha was shaking her head, puzzled.

"*Game* jersey?" she said. "Doesn't he not play anymore?"

"No. He doesn't," Katie said, and her eyes filled with warm tears; so she turned and walked, as fast as she could, out of the lunchroom.

"Wow," Sam said as the girls watched her go. "What do you think happened?"

"I don't know," said Tam. "But I never in my life thought I'd ever hear Katie Henoch talk about childish questions."

"Well," said Hope, "at least there's one thing we don't have to worry about."

The other two searched her face. Hope leaned over the

table. "At least," she said in a loud whisper, "we know it's not about *teenage romance*."

"Right," Tam said, flopping back. "What a relief."

"You guys are kidding, right?" said Sam. "I mean, she's obviously totally plunging."

"Oh, totally," said Hope. "And who knows if there's any water in the pool."

··●··

Katie knew she didn't know that much about him, but she knew one thing. After school, he walked.

So after school today, she waited.

At 2:46 p.m. she stationed herself just inside the doors to the empty lunchroom, just off the main hallway by the front doors, so that everyone passed her but no one would look her way. When she saw her three friends come along the hall, she drew back behind the drink coolers. She hoped he wouldn't pass at the same time. When she looked again, the three heads of the brain trust—Tam's short bouncing hair, Sam's deluxe blond, Hope's long deep brown—were safely by, going through the first set of doors. No sign of him. She resumed watching, half hidden but casual. Hardly anyone even glanced her way.

He came by. He was alone, of course. The hand-grenade silhouette was dark red on his same sweatshirt. She came out into the hall, to follow. Even before he'd stepped through the outer doors, he pulled on his headphones and flipped his hood up over them.

She slipped in among the crowd on the outer patio and saw him turn right toward Grove Street. She walked down the steps and sat on the low wall that ran alongside. She pulled a book from her jacket pocket and pretended to read it as she kept watch. She needed to let him get a safe distance away from all these people.

At the stoplight he turned left onto Grove, toward the city center. Katie stuffed the paperback into her pocket, shouldered her bag, and started to walk.

It was easy to follow unspotted. There were various kids walking in the same direction on the sidewalk. He was taller than the rest, so she could walk normally while also keeping an eye on him. The brain trust had gone off without seeing her. She was clear.

· · ● · ·

If there is a classic old-school American small city, it could be Rutland, Vermont. The big interstate highways never came this way, so for a lot of years the little city didn't change that much. Most people living there can tell you which of the two local high schools, and passionate sports rivals, their parents and grandparents and even great-grandparents attended: either Rutland High, wearers of the red and white, or Mount St. Joseph, MSJ, the local Catholic high school, whose uniforms are green and gold. The basketball rivalry between the two schools ranks second, in noisy shoulder-to-shoulder crowds and bragging rights for the winners, only to football: the Raider and

Mountie football teams have battled each other every single year since 1930. Their game is the biggest event of the year here, and if someone's grandpa happened to score the winning touchdown in, say, 1962, he will have been remembered for that, even defined by that, in Rutland all his life.

The old city center, with its turn-of-the-twentieth-century brick buildings and tall white church steeples, is backed by the high, broad, wooded slopes of the Green Mountains. All through the winter, skiers from the crowded states to the south pass through Rutland on their way up into those mountains. They take interstate highways most of the way, then they drive for an hour on two-lane roads into Rutland. It's a pretty easy drive, just a few hours altogether, and skiers aren't the only ones who make it. These days a steady traffic of cars carrying heroin also comes up from the larger cities to the south, the drug having usually begun its one-way journey north in Mexico or Latin America. The heroin is very potent, and its prices are kept low enough for young people to buy.

And they do. The market in Rutland, as in many other communities across America, is very strong. The local cops, state police, and FBI work together to arrest the drivers who bring the drug up from the south, and also those who sell it here—the local paper is full of these busts, almost every day. But these transporters and local dealers are quickly replaced; the big suppliers stay in the background and rarely get caught. So the one-way traffic flows on, from south to north, and Rutland—like so many other American cities and towns—is a place full of hardworking people who love their kids and their sports, but is also a place with a whole lot of lost souls, most of them young and not long out of school. Like Neal Shaw.

In its struggling and somewhat faded neighborhoods close to the city center—in Katie's neighborhood, where she and Matt were walking now—the drug traffic was so prevalent that Katie, who seemed so innocent, and basically was, could point out the houses and hiding places where the dealing went on. Her own small building, an old home cut into three apartments, was not one of those places.

Katie's mom worked as a cashier at the Price Chopper in the city center. She was as clean as Katie—she didn't even drink, and she worked very hard for her daughter and herself. The squabbling and battling that was so nearly constant between the two these days was mainly about Katie's mom not wanting Katie to make the same mistakes she had. She wanted Katie to have a good life. Katie knew that, but she wanted to have her *own* life. She didn't want to be protected and monitored by her mom and Mrs. Prescott, the older lady downstairs who watched out for Katie while her mom was at work and made sure she had no visitors at all. Katie did not want to be lectured all the time about not letting your opportunities be snatched away by some guy who's just out for himself and can't be counted on, just like—as she had heard far, far too many times—Katie's dad couldn't be counted on, and what had he ever given either of them?

Katie knew her mom was trying. She knew her mom wanted Katie to have more than a small apartment on a dismal street with no money to spare. Katie knew she *would* have a better life, too, but she had to find it for herself. She had to have her own adventures, and it was about time she started. This one was all about him.

· · ● · ·

There is a Stewart's convenience store on the corner of Grove and State streets, near the new courthouse in Rutland. It's one of the older chain convenience stores, a low square brick building with gas pumps out front. Matt didn't decide to walk up to Stewart's, he just did. In the window was a big cutout of an ice-cream cone. The ice-cream part was colored purple. Matt wondered what kind of ice cream was ever purple, and that led to him being inside and staring down at the various rows of metal hatch covers below the ice-cream counter, then looking up at the list of flavors on the wall.

He couldn't remember the last time he'd bought ice cream. He probably wasn't going to this time. It wasn't a wintertime thing, or even much of a springtime thing—and he wasn't much of an ice-cream person anyway. Not these days. But this question of what flavor could be purple intrigued him. Probably nothing, he thought. He wondered though.

Okay, well there was black raspberry on the list. That could be purple. He looked down at the metal hatch covers again. The music pulsed in his phones, and he was wondering where was the black raspberry in the tubs beneath those covers, when he felt a tap on his sleeve.

He looked up. There was the Stewart's guy, an older

teenager. The shirts they wore were dark purple. The guy was miming taking off a set of headphones. Matt took his off.

"Get you something, man?" the guy said. "Cone? Shakes are on special."

The guy had a decent way, not fake-smiley or sulky like older teenagers can be when their jobs require them to wait on younger kids.

"I was looking for purple," Matt said.

"Purple, eh?" The guy grinned and started opening hatch covers. "Let's see. Purple."

"I was thinking maybe the black raspberry," Matt said.

"Oh hey, that's right here," the guy said, pointing. "It's more a darkish red, though."

"Kind of purple."

"Well, sure!" The guy straightened up, grinning. "Key to the service business: the customer is always right. That there is purple raspberry. Want some?"

"Ah . . . I don't know."

Another customer was standing by the register. "Well," the guy said, sliding in that direction, "let me know if you decide."

"Why purple?" said another voice, on Matt's other side.

Matt looked, and there was a girl. She had brown hair and was looking at the flavors. She looked up at him, and she was nice-looking. But she seemed a little nervous or something.

"Well, that thing in the window, that big cone thing—the ice-cream part is purple," Matt said. "It sort of made me wonder what real ice cream is ever that color."

The girl nodded. She seemed to be pondering.

"Maybe a grape?" she asked.

"Hmm. Yeah," Matt said. "I don't think they have grape though."

They were both looking at the flavor list now. Matt shook his head. "Yeah, well, anyway . . ." He started to go.

"You know what I notice?" the girl said quickly.

"What?"

"Well . . . it's like there's two kinds of flavors."

"Sure—ice cream and frozen yogurt. It's right up there."

"But if you look at it a different way," the girl said. "There's flavors like, okay, cotton candy. Chocolate marshmallow. Brownie fudge M&M. I mean, what do those flavors say to you?"

"Attention deficit hyperactivity disorder?"

She smiled delightedly at him. She had sort of vibrating, happy eyes. "Well, basically, yeah," she said. "Now, there are certain other flavors. Pecan," she said, dropping her voice low and talking slowly. "But-ter pecan. Fat-free rainbow sherbet. And, of course . . . va . . . nilla."

The way she intoned "vanilla" made him almost laugh. Almost. He said, "I get it—grownup flavors. Kid flavors and grownup flavors."

She nodded, looking into his eyes. "Don't you think?"

"Yeah, but I think there's some that bridge the gap. Like . . . chocolate peanut butter cup."

"Hmm," she said. "Good point. What about chocolate chip cookie dough?"

He didn't say anything. A feeling came over him.

She looked up. There was an awkward silence. Finally she said, "A lot of people have memories of eating cookie dough. As a kid and stuff."

He didn't answer.

"I mean," she said, "you hardly ever ate it alone, right? It wasn't something you just went and had. You had it because somebody was making you cookies. Right?"

She seemed to be trying, for some reason, trying in a gentle sort of way—but he didn't want this. He nodded and turned away.

"I got to go," he said, and pushed open the door.

He was walking down State Street and was just putting his phones back on when he heard: "Wait."

He turned. The girl was catching up. She was holding each hand out, and up, in a funny way. He held his phones out from his ears.

"I got you one," she said, coming up, looking very serious. But both of her hands, as she held them out, were empty. Her fingers were curved as if she had an ice-cream cone in each hand, but she didn't. It was odd.

He let his phones fall around his neck.

"What's up?" he said.

She took a breath. "Nothing," she said. "I just thought you might like one. It can be that flavor, or color—that purple, if you want. It can be any flavor." She held out the imaginary cone again.

"I don't get it," he said.

"It's a void cone," she said.

His breath caught. He looked at her. She looked right straight back.

He didn't reach out for the void cone, but he didn't put his phones back on either. He turned away and started walking. After a few steps he turned back. She was still standing there, one hand still out. She was looking down at the sidewalk now.

"Well?" he said. "You coming or not?"

WARM HANDS

They walked away from Stewart's, away from school, away from Grove Street. Neither one had any idea what to say now. When Matt just walked and didn't say anything, Katie looked up at him nervously. She was afraid to see him put his headphones back on, but he didn't. He just kept striding and she scooted along, keeping up with quick scissoring steps.

They were walking through a back section of the old downtown, with a neighborhood of small, faded houses behind it. They walked by a bakery, a tiny old pizza place, a gas station turned into a gun shop, an addiction recovery center, and a combination laundromat and tanning parlor called Wash 'n' Glow. Then they were beyond the back end of the business district and were walking past the regional correctional center, the prison with its high brick outer walls. Past that they were in a neighborhood of nicer homes, and still Matt said nothing. Katie kept looking up at him. Her mind was flickering nervously. Would he ever say anything?

Finally she realized: *He's waiting for me to explain. I need to explain, don't I?*

"It was a total accident," she said. "I mean what happened. Well, maybe it wasn't a total accident but it was totally unplanned. I mean, maybe it wasn't just random—it might have been meant to happen, or something, in some way—but it *did* just happen."

She thought, *Oh great. Even I have no idea what I'm trying to say.* What could he possibly be thinking? He was just walking along, not looking at her.

She took a deep breath and stopped walking. A pace or two ahead, he stopped, too, and turned back.

"I know you think I spied on you, or that I set you up or something," Katie said, "but I absolutely, totally, honestly did not. I was just in that chat room like you. Because I had questions, you know? Not questions about you. I didn't know you. I just . . . had questions. Just like you, I think. Yes?"

He nodded.

Yes, thought Katie.

"So . . . well," she said, "I mean we seemed to hit it off so well, just right away, and we were talking about *real things*, you know? And I could tell you were a guy, so it was different. I mean, my friends I can talk with, I mean we really do talk, but to be talking with a guy that way . . ."

She pleaded silently for him to say something, to help her out in some way before she just gibbered on and on into helplessness. But he just nodded again and jammed his hands into his jean pockets. He looked at the sidewalk.

"It was different," he said finally. "I mean for me, too. I never talked to anybody. Not about stuff like that."

"Not anybody?"

"Not really." He squinted at her for a second, then looked right down again. It wasn't true, exactly. But he was not about to mention Neal.

"It's important to talk," she said gently. "It's good to talk." When he didn't answer she tried again. "Everybody needs to talk."

Still looking down, he shrugged.

After a long moment she said, "Well . . . anyway, I don't know where we're going, but let's keep going, okay?"

He smiled, and her heart popped up. They began walking again, and as they walked she explained in a rush: "When we were in that room it was you who said you lived in Vermont and went to Jeffords. I definitely didn't know that. I mean, how could I? Anybody in a chat room could be from anywhere. My friends tell me not to go near them, but this one felt okay to me. And that night it was just us, it happened to be only us two— and you said something about being a ninth-grader at Jeffords, and then I was just like, Who *is* this guy? Because suddenly I knew you were at *my* school, and that was so amazing. Of course I wondered who you were, so I asked if you had any, you know, activities or interests or anything—and you said that about playing basketball but not anymore. And when I asked if you were bad at it you said no you were really good at it. And then I knew."

He looked over at her. He started to smile.

"That was it?" he said.

"Yes! That was it. I couldn't help knowing who you were, at that point, and the next day when I came into school in the morning, there you were. Do you remember? I mean it was just you and me, and that was so kind of amazing."

Now she blushed. She thought she had gone too far, said too much. But she looked at him and he was still smiling.

"I remember that," he said.

"You do?" Her heart was jumping.

"Yeah." But he didn't say more.

"Well," she said. "Yeah. So, okay. That night we were going to talk. To IM. We'd already planned it. And, I mean, I wasn't trying to hide who I was—you just never asked. You could have clicked up my IM bio, right? You could have found out."

He squinted. "You can do that?"

"Of course you can! Haven't you posted an IM bio?"

He shrugged. "I don't really do IM. I just did it that time because you wanted to."

"Huh," she said. "Well, anyway, when I saw you that morning before school . . . I mean . . . I just felt that was really meaningful. And then that night we were talking *so* well, and when you said that thing about not trusting anybody ever because someone could break your heart or sell their soul or something, well I just felt so *bad* for you. And I said your name. But that was it, you know? That's all it was. There was no spying or setting up or anything. That's really all it was. It was just 'cause I felt bad for you."

They were walking up a hill now, past houses, and she was

breathing hard and fast. Despite the steepness, they had sped up. She suddenly realized how fast they were walking.

"Hey," she said. "Can we slow down or rest or something? Just for a second?"

He stopped, and he saw her as if for the first time. She was breathing hard and her eyes were open wide, looking up at him. Her eyes were so brown and warm, and her whole face was so *nice*-looking that he felt a wave of warmness and longing roll through him. He wanted to kiss her, right then, and something told him he probably could . . . but he didn't know how. He didn't know the move.

But he was amazed that her story made sense, that suddenly it was okay that this had happened, and it was okay that here they were. He felt like he knew her. Like he could joke around with her. But he didn't. Instead he said, "Okay?"

He meant, was she okay to walk.

She understood. She smiled shyly and said yes, and the feeling rolled right through him again, and this time it poured from him toward her. It was so strong that he had to do something, so as he turned to start walking again he reached for her hand. She wove her fingers quickly and warmly through his. And they walked, their fingers meshed and their hands palm to palm, warming together.

· · ● · ·

That afternoon it seemed to both Matt and Katie as if their lives before had been gray, shadowed under some heavy blanket of clouds, and now the sun was out and you could see so much. You could see everything, in the warm, bright, brand-new light. Which was funny, because neither one remembered much about what they saw that afternoon, nor many other details except that this was how it felt. They just walked and walked, and sometimes they talked and sometimes they didn't; they just kept going, and neither one noticed where or felt tired. There was just the excitement and the warmness that passed through their hands, which they never let go. Neither would chance letting go that clasp and breaking the spell.

Katie told Matt about her mother and how they didn't get along anymore. She found herself saying that she knew her mom did want her to have a good life, but she needed to have her *own* life and why couldn't her mom see that? And she told about her dad, what she knew about him, how her mom had said he'd never been the same after the war, though he wasn't really that great before the war either. Neither of them had heard from him in years. They didn't expect to.

Matt listened as she told him about Tam, Sam, and Hope—about each of the girls in turn, and how great they were and how close they'd been until now. Then Katie took a breath and talked about feeling like there was something she couldn't talk to her friends about right now. She struggled to explain how it seemed to have to do with feeling smothered by their tight little group. She wanted room to breathe, or something. Did that make any sense? Did Matt understand? He nodded and held her hand, and she felt that he did understand.

Matt talked some about his family, too. He said his dad was

a doctor and an important one, a cardiologist, and he was incredibly busy. He was really well regarded, and he was involved with a lot of different stuff. Matt said this somewhat proudly, but also vaguely. He said his mom sold houses, real estate, and she basically lived in her SUV. She'd zoom in to get dinner on the table, most days she did do that, then she'd zoom out again and be off showing houses or at the meetings and groups and projects that you had to be involved with if you wanted to be a well-known and successful part of your community and make it a better place. Katie felt that Matt was saying what he was expected to say, but that there was something more behind it, as if he wasn't totally okay with how things were. But he wasn't saying that. He said, again, that his parents were very involved with the community.

"They must be so proud of you guys," Katie said.

"Umm," said Matt, sort of grunting.

"I know your brother was really well known."

"Umm."

"Tell me about him," Katie said as they walked.

"Uh? Who?"

"Who. Your brother, that's who." She squeezed his hand. He didn't squeeze back.

"I don't know."

"I used to see his picture in the paper," she said. "In the sports section."

He nodded. "He was a good ballplayer."

"Was? Doesn't he play anymore?"

"Not right now."

"What does he do?"

"I don't know, okay?" Matt said that sharply and it was the first sharp or odd thing he'd said or done. She clung to his hand, which had gone limp like he wanted to be let go.

"I'm sorry," she said. "I didn't mean to make anything weird."

"It's not weird," he said.

"Well, it seems . . ."

"It's just family stuff, okay? Just let it go."

"Okay," she said, and now she knew she was not to ask any questions about that. Even though she was a questioner by nature, Katie accepted this right away because she wanted the warmth and the closeness back. Right away.

"Okay," she said. And she changed the subject and gradually, as they talked about anything but family, his hand rewarmed and folded into hers again, and she believed everything was all right.

· • ● • ·

It was getting late and they were walking down the same hill that they'd walked up when she was first trying to explain. It had been so great, this whole time, but now there was the feeling that each step was bringing them closer to the end of it, to saying goodbye. Katie wanted to know she had something she could hold on to. She said, "I feel like we're supposed to be here. Like this was all supposed to happen."

"Yeah?"

"I do," she said. He smiled, and she walked closer so their shoulders touched. She wanted him to put his arm around her, but he didn't. Still they were walking very close, and she knew they felt close, too.

Matt wanted to tell her how it had been for him—how through all the long, gray afternoons before this, all those times of walking these streets before she'd come along, he had felt and thought that nothing much made sense. That nothing had much meaning at all. He would see people doing ordinary things and he'd think, *Why would they do those things?* Whatever it was, he would think, *How empty must that be? Why do that over and over and over till you die?* It was like nothing at all seemed worth doing, or that anything anybody could do— anything he could possibly do—would just be so useless and pointless and empty.

He wanted to tell her how that had felt. He almost tried to. He knew she would have listened, and asked him questions, and felt really bad for him. But he didn't want her to feel bad. And this was so different, the way this felt right now, being with her on these same streets, that all those gray, wintry afternoons before felt like they hadn't happened at all. They were gone, and so was the empty pointless feeling. He wanted to tell her how it felt to be with her, but he didn't want to mess it up by talking about it; so he just held her hand and breathed and looked around. It was all so totally different.

Matt really liked how she talked. She was so full of life and so enthusiastic, and he really liked just looking at her. He liked the way her hair swung off her shoulders as she walked and talked, and how her cheeks were flushed and her eyes danced around and then took him in. He really liked it when she looked at him that way, like she was wrapping him in the warmth of her eyes. She talked about all kinds of stuff—people in school, kids and their silly crushes and breakups and dramas, and things she'd heard about people that they both couldn't believe were true. Matt held her hand tightly the whole time. In a way, he wanted to do more, but he was also very happy just like this. He hadn't felt happy in a long time.

When the afternoon light was very low and they were down off the hill and walking into the old back end of downtown, toward Stewart's at last, Katie began feeling all the tiredness in her ankles and her legs. She was holding on, not wanting this to end. She wanted to say just the right thing.

As they came onto the convenience store's little corner lot, she had to say something.

"Matt," she said.

"Uh-huh?" They stopped, and he faced her.

She hesitated. "It's . . . well . . ." She wasn't sure what she would say. Something. "You can trust me," she said.

Matt let go her hand. He nodded, but he didn't look at her.

"I know people have been . . . you know . . . I mean making judgments about you and stuff," Katie said. God, that sounded stupid. But she had to keep trying: "I mean, because you stopped playing when people wanted you to. I just want you to know that whatever's going on . . . it's okay with me."

He nodded. He looked at her for only a flicker of a second. "Sure," he said. "That's cool."

But that wasn't enough, it didn't feel like enough, and suddenly she wasn't sure about anything. *Did* he trust her? Would he call? Did he want to do something again? Did he really feel the same?

"I want to do this again," he said. The warm light leaped inside Katie.

"You do?"

"Yeah. Definitely."

"How about tomorrow?"

"Tomorrow is good," he said.

"Will you call me tonight?"

"Sure."

"On the phone, not IM. So I can hear you. Okay?" She took both his hands.

"Yeah." He smiled, and they hesitated for a moment, facing each other. There was a suspended uncertainty. Then Matt said, awkwardly, "So . . . I mean, are you walking home?"

"Oh. Sure."

"Which way?"

"Oh!" She realized they didn't know where each other lived. "I'm just off Grove Street. A little ways up."

"Yeah? I'm up Grove, too."

"Really!"

"Yeah." He seemed happy, too, and when they got to Katie's apartment house and she said this was it, there was no more awkwardness. He squeezed her hand and said, "See you tomorrow."

"After school," she said.

He nodded. "That'd be good," he said.

"But you're going to call later, right?"

"Sure. Bye." He left kind of quickly, and Katie understood that he wanted to kiss her but wasn't sure how or if it would be okay right there. She went inside floating on a feeling of esteem and belonging like she'd never had before in her life.

As Matt walked home—and it was a fairly long walk, all the way from her neighborhood out to his—he felt like he had it all back. He had the flow back, the very best of it, the awareness of yourself as magically moving in an energy where you were totally appreciated and you totally belonged and nothing could go wrong. It lasted until he walked up his driveway and saw the police car.

EMPTY SPACE

Matt froze. His mind locked up. He still had that glow inside him, the warm humming energy of keeping an incredible secret, but as he walked toward the front door, step by step the other secret began to take hold again. He had to keep his expression blank. Tell them nothing. But what if something had happened that was really, really bad? What if Neal was not okay, then what would he tell them?

He noticed there was no ambulance. Only a cop car. That might be a good sign—or at least a less bad one. When he pushed open the front door, hearing its tiny creak, there were already too many secrets inside him, and he had no idea what would be inside his house.

He heard his dad's voice. "Matthew?" His dad shouldn't be home so soon. It wasn't even dark.

"Is that you, honey?" called his mom. "We're in the living room."

Matt came to the living room, where no one in his family

was normally allowed to go, except for holidays just before dinner when relatives came over and everyone perched on chairs, or when his parents had cocktail parties. Perched in there today were his dad, his mom, and a police officer.

"Hello, son," his dad said gravely, and nodded toward a chair they had brought in from the dining room. Matt saw a depression in its padded yellow-and-white-striped seat, and he guessed that Neal had just been sitting there. If so, he was gone now. They had talked to him already, and they'd been waiting for Matt. In a way, Matt thought, that was good. If Neal *could* talk to them, and if he had satisfied them enough to be let go, and if there hadn't been an ambulance, yes that was probably good. Also Neal hadn't been in the backseat of the cop car, in handcuffs. Unless there had been another cop car . . .

"Matthew, please sit down," his dad said.

Matt sat.

His parents were huddled together on the couch. The cop sat on a chair beside them, his blue hat on the coffee table. He had a notepad in his lap. He also had a really thick, droopy mustache. It was very dark, almost black. Matt focused on that mustache. It was like he couldn't help it.

"This is Officer Petryka," Matt's dad said. He pronounced it with a long "i" sound in the middle. Officer Petryka nodded at Matt, then turned so Matt could see the nameplate on his uniform shirt.

"Everyone wants to know how to spell it," the cop said, and smiled through his mustache at Matt.

"Son, something has happened," said his dad, resuming control the way he did. "I'll let the officer tell you about it." Matt's mom sat with her hands folded in her lap, with a tight face and hurt eyes. But Matt reminded himself: *No ambulance. Neither parent has rushed to the hospital or anything. So Neal must be okay, right?*

Officer Petryka's mustache lifted as he started to talk. "Matt," he said, "there have been a series of thefts from your house."

The mustache stopped. Everyone stopped. They were looking at Matt.

"Huh?"

"The first theft appears to have occurred"—the cop glanced at his notebook—"about a month ago. Your mother noticed that a necklace, a gold necklace with an amethyst pendant, was missing from her jewelry box." Matt was wondering what the difference was between a necklace and a pendant when the mustache started moving again.

"She thought she might have misplaced it," the cop said, and looked at his mom. His mom nodded, her hurt eyes on Matt. The cop said, "She didn't mention it to anyone, hoping the necklace would turn up."

The cop glanced again at his pad. "Then last week, a keepsake watch that your father inherited from his father, a gold-plated Hamilton, was noticed missing by your father from his box on top of his dresser. Are you familiar with the box I'm referring to?"

The cop was looking at Matt. Everyone was.

"I don't know," Matt said. "I guess."

"All right. Now, again," the cop said, "no report was made. In fact, for a time your dad didn't mention this to your mom, because he too was hoping the watch would turn up, even though he did not wear it and had no reason to think he had misplaced it."

Matt's parents were holding hands now. His dad's mouth was tight.

"I guess I didn't want to think what might have happened," his dad said. He shook his head.

"Then, today," the cop resumed, "your mother came home from work and found that your father's Kenmore stereo amplifier was gone. This was clearly no accident or oversight. Your mom called your dad at work, and they shared that each had previously noticed a valuable item of their own missing. They had not previously discussed those missing items. It now appears clear that there has been a series of thefts from your house."

The mustache stopped moving. Matt looked from it to his mom and dad's held hands. He looked up: they were all watching him closely. He wondered why.

"Matt," the cop said as he pulled his pen out of his shirt pocket and clicked it, preparing to write in his notebook. "What did you do after school today?"

Now Matt realized why. Heat flushed up through him and he felt himself go red, then he realized how that must look. His mom's eyes were agonized.

"I just walked around," Matt said.

The cop made a note. "Were you alone?"

Matt hesitated.

"Matthew," his dad said evenly.

"Yeah," Matt said.

"You were alone," the cop said.

"Yes." Matt felt a prickling down his face and chest. He wondered: Could he and Katie be found out? Had anyone seen them? But how could he say anything? How could he tell them about Katie right now? If he did tell them he was with her, then he'd have to tell the cop her name, and the cop would call her mom, and . . . no.

"I always just walk by myself," Matt said.

"Can you tell me where you went?" asked the cop.

"Well . . . I went out State Street," Matt said. "Past the correctional center. Up into those neighborhoods. I just walked around up there."

The cop nodded, scribbling. He looked up. "Your parents say you're pretty much out on your own every afternoon. Are you always by yourself?"

"Yes."

"No particular friends you hang out with, places you go?"

"No," Matt said. "I just walk."

"Every day?" The cop was studying him.

"Yes," Matt said, slipping into the stubbornness he had built up and strengthened through the long, lonely winter of refusing to explain.

"I just walk," he said, straightening up and looking the cop in the eye. "I like to walk."

"Is there anyone who could verify what you were doing today, where you were? Anyone you spoke to, or visited with?"

"No . . . Yeah! There was a kid in Stewart's. We talked about ice cream. Flavors. He works there." This was perfect, Matt thought. It was before Katie, so it would be perfect.

"Did you buy some ice cream?"

"Well . . . no. But we talked about it."

The cop nodded. Matt's dad's mouth was tight again and he shook his head a little, looking at the coffee table. Matt saw that his dad didn't believe him.

"You could ask him," Matt said quickly. "He'd remember, 'cause we were talking about purple ice cream. If any flavors are purple. He had kind of short, sort of curly hair. And glasses. A high school kid, I think. You could ask him."

"All right," the cop said. He made another note, then looked up at Matt. "Have there been any people here at the house, during the day, that you are unfamiliar with or who seemed in any way, you know, suspicious to you?"

Matt shrugged. He hesitated. Everyone was looking at him.

"I'm not here very much," he said.

"Is that a no?" said the cop.

Matt shrugged again. "I'm just not here," he mumbled.

His dad said, "Matthew, we'd like a straight answer, please."

Matt sat up and looked at the cop. "I don't know any suspicious characters hanging around here," he said in a very straight way. It was true, too. He didn't know any of them.

Finally the cop said, "Okay." He closed his notebook and turned to Matt's mom and dad. "We'll be in touch soon."

Matt's parents stood up, the cop stood up, and his dad shook the cop's hand. The cop shook Matt's hand and looked once more into his eyes. Then at last the cop left, and the Shaw family, minus one brother, was left standing there.

"Let me show you something," his dad said, and he walked out of the room. Matt knew he was expected to follow, and he did.

His dad walked into the family room and stopped by the home entertainment center, by the big flat-screen TV and the tall CD tower. He glanced downward and Matt, following his gaze, saw the empty space on the white shelf, second one from the bottom, where the expensive black amp had been. He saw some wires back there, lying unconnected. Matt looked around the room; it seemed like nothing else had been disturbed. Matt wondered why just the one thing.

"Matthew," his dad said quietly. "What the hell is going on?"

Matt shook his head. "I don't know," he said, though he had a pretty good idea. "It wasn't me," he said, which was true. His dad kept staring at him. "I don't know anything about it, Dad. I don't," Matt said, though that wasn't true. He was shocked and stunned, but he knew. He knew. He didn't know for sure if it was Neal or one of Neal's loser friends, but he knew.

"It wasn't me, Dad," Matt said as his dad turned to walk away.

· · ● · ·

Matt suffered through his usual dinner at the kitchen table. His mom set his plate down, then sat in the chair beside him. She looked at him with those mournful eyes.

In a low voice, even though no one else was in the kitchen to hear, she said, "Is there anything you want to tell me?"

Matt frowned at his pork chop. He shook his head.

"I didn't do anything," he said. "I don't know anything about it. I don't."

His mom looked at him for a long time. Outside and on the phone, at work and with friends, she was always chattering, always charming; but at home she worked a lot with long silences. Matt knew to wait them out, to stay relaxed.

"Well," she finally said. "I trust you. I do. I've never had any reason not to trust you. I just don't know what to think. There was no sign of forced entry. The officer asked mainly about you boys."

"Both of us?"

"Yes. Why?"

Matt realized he'd asked something meaningful. He just shrugged, went blank, and ate mashed potato.

Finally his mother stood up, hugging herself tight. "It's so strange," she said, not really to Matt. "So strange not to feel safe. In your own home."

· · ● · ·

Matt was doing homework at about eight when his phone rang, and that jangled him. He'd been trying to focus on the work and shut everything else out.

"Hi," Katie said.

After a second he said, "Hey."

"Is . . . everything okay? We talked about you calling," she said. "Did you remember? Or no?"

"Oh," Matt said. "I . . . kind of didn't. Sorry about that. My bad."

"It's okay," she said, but her voice was quiet.

"I was just into homework," he offered, knowing that was lame, but having no other thoughts about how to handle this. He had totally forgotten.

"What subjects do you have?" she asked. He understood that she meant his homework, and he told her. They chatted for a minute. She seemed to be okay. So then he said, "Hey, you know, the thing is, I really need to do this."

"Oh. Well . . ."

"No offense," he said.

"It's okay. I should be working, too. So. Tomorrow?"

"Uh . . . yeah."

There was a silence.

"Are you sure everything's okay?" she asked.

"Well, actually it's a little weird tonight." He heard her breath catch, and quickly said: "It's not you. It's just family stuff. No big deal."

"Oh. Well, if you want to talk . . ."

"I really should do this work."

"Okay. Tomorrow after school?"

Matt thought a second. "Yeah, but not at school. Over at Stewart's, okay? I can meet you there."

"Well . . . okay." Katie sounded disappointed, or confused. But to Matt it was important to just have his privacy, the privacy of walking away from school on his own as usual, not giving people who didn't know anything something new to whisper about. He wanted to keep things private. Secure.

At her end, Katie could tell something was wrong, but she stopped herself from asking questions. "All right," she said carefully. Then she added, "I can't wait," and listened closely for the response.

"Uh . . . sure," Matt said. "Same here. Bye," and he hung up.

Katie wanted to cry, and wasn't sure why. All kinds of questions and uncertainties were half forming and felt urgent inside her. She looked at the phone in her hand for a while. Then she dialed Tamra.

· · ● · ·

Later that night, Matt stepped outdoors through the garage. He walked along the back patio and knocked on his brother's outside door.

No music boomed from inside. At night, if he was here and their parents were around, Neal kept things very quiet. He was very good at attracting no suspicion.

Neal opened the door a crack—and Matt stuck one foot, in its winter-worn and dirty basketball shoe, in the crack. Neal tried to jam the door shut, but couldn't. Matt stood there, waiting.

Now Neal sighed and opened the door. Matt stepped inside.

He hadn't been in here for months. It smelled close, like it hadn't been aired out in a while. It was dark in Neal's room except for the TV's flickering, changing light that played across his couch and bed. The bed was a mess. The couch had a pillow and a wadded-up blanket on it. Basically the room looked like it always had, with basketball trophies looming atop the bookshelf, in the gloom above the TV light, and CDs in messy drifting piles on the floor. It was basically the same though messier, but it felt different. A pile of empty, crumpled-up candy wrappers and cookie bags had been tossed in the corner on the floor. Between the TV and the couch, with a mess everywhere else, Neal's coffee table was empty, like it had been cleaned off.

Neal walked back to the couch, scratching his neck, and lay down. The TV light played on his face as he stared at it, ignoring Matt. He didn't say anything. His face was empty. Matt sat on the coffee table.

"What did you tell them?" Matt asked.

For a couple seconds Neal didn't answer, like he hadn't heard. Then he shrugged.

"Not much to tell," he said, scratching the inside of his elbow through his long-sleeved T-shirt.

Matt stared. Neal just looked sleepily at the TV. He yawned. He had dark circles under his eyes, and his face was skinnier than ever. It was pimply, too. Neal had never had pimples before.

"You can't do this," Matt said.

Neal finally looked up at him. "Hey, you know what?" he said, and very slowly yawned. "They're worried about you."

"What?"

Neal shrugged, gazing back at the TV. "Oh yeah," he said as the colors played on his face. "They think you're strange. Antisocial. They asked me about it. They don't know where you go. It seems a little"—he gazed at Matt through half-closed eyes—"suspicious."

"Neal. You can't do this."

"Do what? I told them I didn't know anything. You should thank me, dude."

Matt felt heat fill his face. "What about you? What about what you're doing?" It was the closest he had ever come to asking.

Neal closed his eyes.

"I'm taking a little time off," he said, and smiled.

"I can tell them stuff," Matt said.

Neal's eyes opened halfway again. "I don't think so," he said, and closed them. "Nothing to tell."

"I'm not covering for you," Matt said.

"Nah. Hey, dude, it's you they're worried about." Neal smiled. "I'd be careful."

Matt thought: *He needs a new name. He's not Neal anymore.*

Matt stood up to go.

"Couldn't you get some kind of help?" he said.

His brother smiled again, eyes still closed. "I got help," he said. "I got the best help. Now go. And don't come back."

STRAWBERRY
BLONDE

The next day was Friday. Between periods in the early afternoon, Matt was at his locker when KJ stopped by. KJ leaned against the next locker, and he spoke softly as chatting and clamoring kids flowed past.

"Hey," KJ said.

"Hey."

"Hey, so . . . I don't know if it's cool to ask this, but . . ."

"What?"

"At your house. Yesterday."

"Yeah?"

"Well, the cop car. There was a cop car."

"Oh. Yeah."

"I could see it from my driveway," KJ said. "I was out shooting. It was there for a while. Right out front."

"I know where it was," Matt said, his head in his locker.

"Yeah. Well . . ." KJ looked around to make sure no one

else was close or was listening. "I just wondered if, you know, everything's okay for you."

"If everything's okay for *me*?" Matt slammed his locker door; KJ's head snapped back. "Why should something not be okay for me?"

"Hey, jeez, chill, okay? I just wondered."

"Oh yeah. You wondered if I'm doing something everybody can buzz about. Like they did all winter. Well, I'm not. Okay? I wasn't then and I'm not now."

"Hey, you know what? I never buzzed," KJ said. "I never asked you, I never talked to anyone about it, I never got in your business. Not once. I'm trying to help, that's all. If you don't want it . . ."

"I don't need it."

"Okay. Cool," KJ said, and he walked away.

Matt watched him going down the hall, a stubby boy with a determined, head-down way of walking. Matt knew it was true—KJ hadn't been part of the whispering that had spread all over the school when Matt wouldn't play and wouldn't say why. Matt realized now that KJ had never asked him about it, not at all. The boys lived next door to each other; they had known each other forever. They had played youth ball together. KJ could have pried, or even spied. But he never had.

Matt remembered those years of youth ball. From fourth grade through sixth, he and KJ had played together on their elementary school team. Back then, when size and skills were less developed and mattered less than pure effort and fearlessness,

99

KJ had been the bulldog guard, the full-steam-ahead kid who would take the ball straight at anybody. It didn't matter who. He had a low center of gravity and he would leave people sprawling, out-racing and out-diving anyone for any loose ball. KJ was always the most fearless kid on the court, and he was fun to play with. But he wasn't really built for the game, and by seventh grade the game had passed him by. But, still, Matt knew who KJ was.

Matt had been so caught up in his own struggle that he hadn't thought much about who his real friends were, if he still had any. Now he felt bad. He stuffed that feeling down where he had been stuffing all the things he felt worried or scared about, because he didn't know what to do about any of them. He walked to class.

·· ● ··

Katie still wasn't sure what to feel or think about Matt wanting to meet at Stewart's, blocks away from school. Was he just shy? Was he embarrassed about being seen together or maybe holding hands in front of other kids? Or was it something worse? Like maybe that he had seen where she lived and realized she was basically poor, and maybe he didn't want to be seen with her now. Could that be it? He came from a really successful family, she knew that. Why did her tiny little family and apartment and everything have to be so . . . pathetic?

She felt torn and guilty for even thinking that. But what if it was what Matt was thinking? But, she thought, how much could he know? How much had she told? Not that much, so far. She had said her mom worked at the Price Chopper, and some other stuff. She didn't know what would happen if Matt knew all about them . . . But if she lied, she'd be lying about her *family*.

When she had talked to Tam last night about Matt, Tam had listened, then told her to be careful.

"You just don't know about him," Tam had said. "Nobody does."

"He's just private," Katie had said. "Or shy."

"Maybe," Tam had said, "but you don't really know. All I'm saying is, be careful. Don't get all swept away, don't just plunge. All right?"

Katie had sighed. "All right," she'd said, wondering why everything had to get so complicated so fast.

All day at school Katie hadn't seen Matt, and she didn't know how to handle those moments that were coming after 2:45, when school would get out. Should she rush to Stewart's and wait for him? Or should she march up to him right outside school and say, "Let's go"? She almost wanted to do that, to show him she didn't accept being told what to do. But what if he got furious and stalked away? What if he *was* ashamed of her? What if he didn't really like her—or what if he was one of those guys who, if they liked you, they couldn't stand it and they had to treat you like dirt?

Katie writhed in this torment all day. She didn't talk about it with anyone; she shied away from everyone. She didn't want to say anything that might make Matt look bad, when she really didn't know what he was thinking and everyone already seemed to have some uninformed judgment about him. Even saying "Nobody knows him, nobody knows what's going on with him" was a kind of judgment, wasn't it? Saying that assumed that what was going on with him must be something dark and bad.

Katie finally decided that the best thing to do right after school was just what she would normally do. If she was normally going to walk to Stewart's to meet someone, which she had actually never done before, but if she was she would walk out of school and head down the street. Just as she had yesterday, she would turn left at the Grove Street light and walk toward the city center.

She didn't get that far. She came down the front steps, grateful not to have seen her friends and so have to explain or justify anything, when she spotted Matt. He was already down the street a ways, walking on the far side. Next she saw a woman, an adult woman with thick strawberry-blond hair, step out of a dark-blue car parked across the street and casually greet Matt. He stopped. Katie couldn't see his face, but the strawberry-blond woman was talking to him in what seemed a friendly way. Matt seemed to listen, though his head was mostly down.

Katie stepped back a bit, so she was partly hidden by a tree at the corner of the school's front steps. She sat on a step and watched. The woman and Matt began to walk together down the street. Then Matt stopped, so the woman stopped, too. They stood there in front of the gray stone synagogue by the corner, and they talked—or the woman talked—for some time.

Then the woman pulled something small and white out of her pocket and held it out. Matt took it and stuck it in his pocket. A strange, confusing feeling came over Katie, a feeling that she did not understand at all.

$$\cdot \ \cdot \ \bullet \ \cdot \ \cdot$$

When the woman stepped out of the car, smiled at him, and said, "Hi, Matt Shaw?," it was almost like she had just said someone else's name. Matt didn't even nod. She pulled out a wallet, let it fall open to a gold-colored badge, then quickly put it away. She stuck her hands in her pockets.

"I'm Detective Carolyn Casey from the Rutland City Police," she said. "Mind if I walk with you for just a few steps?"

Matt didn't move. The woman said, "Matt, you're not in trouble. I just wanted to connect with you. Obviously something's going on, with these thefts from your house, and it's my job to try to learn what it might be. I'd just like to know who you are, a little bit, and have you know me. Can we walk for just a minute?"

Matt shrugged and started to walk. The detective said, "I've been asking around a bit today, 'cause that's my job. Seems like a lot of people are all, 'Ooh, what's going on with this Matt kid,' because you wouldn't play ball this year. That must have been kind of a pain, I mean getting attitude from people just 'cause you're going through some changes."

Matt stopped. He said, "You don't need to try to talk like a kid, okay? You're not actually that good at it."

Detective Casey smiled—a big, surprising smile. She was fairly pretty actually, in a thick-haired, freckle-faced kind of way. Matt thought she looked like she'd been a girl jock in school.

"You got me," she said. "We learn that in detective school. It's just about trying to relate to people. How would you like me to talk to you?"

Matt shrugged. "It doesn't matter," he said. "There's really not anything to talk about."

"That's what I heard—that you don't want to talk," she said. "I talked to the coach. He said he couldn't tell me much of anything, because you wouldn't tell him anything. He really doesn't get it. I talked to the school safety officer, Officer Castilliano? He said you're basically a well-liked kid, but you've kind of cut yourself off from people. He said people don't really know what you do with yourself these days."

Matt just looked at her. He didn't like this.

"Well," she said, "the thing is, Matt, those are some of the things that people who care about kids can worry about. When we learn about things we should worry about, kind of danger signs, they can include stuff like suddenly giving up favorite activities, suddenly cutting off contact with friends, not explaining what a person is doing with his free time. Stuff like that. It doesn't mean you're in trouble with us—I want you to understand that. But it does indicate to me that, you know, something may be going on. In your life. Or in your family, maybe."

Matt flushed. "I'm just walking around," he said quickly. "I'm not doing anything wrong."

The detective nodded, looking closely at him. "You know, I go a lot by first impressions," she said. "I think you're a good kid. I look in your eyes and, to be honest, they look clear. But I also feel like you're bothered by something, Matt. Maybe it's a feeling I get, or maybe it's what I'm thinking after talking with people, after learning about the changes in your behavior, and now meeting you."

She stared down at the street for a few seconds, like she was trying to decide how to say something.

"Seems like you've cut yourself off, Matt. You know? What I'm feeling is, if you're such a good ballplayer—and people say you're excellent, by the way—but now you won't play anymore, and if everyone says you're a decent kid but now you won't hang out or talk with your friends anymore, then I feel like something might really be troubling you. I don't know. Maybe it's something you're scared to talk about, or something you don't know what to do about. Kids do get into situations like that. You'd be surprised how often I see something like that. I don't jump to any conclusions at all. But I do see the signs that tell me something's maybe going on, in some way. Or something's wrong. You see what I mean?"

Matt shrugged. He looked down.

"Well," she said. "I just wanted to meet you, and introduce myself. I'd like to ask if I can give you my card. Um, oh—here it is." She pulled one hand from her pocket, holding the card.

She acted casual, like she'd just happened to find it, but Matt knew she knew what she was doing. Still, he didn't have a bad feeling about her. He took the card and stuck it in his jeans pocket.

"Matt, I have to look into these thefts from your house," the detective said. "That's my job. I often get assigned to situations that involve families, because, you know, I like families. I come from a Rutland family, went to MSJ. In fact I have a cousin at Jeffords. I think he's in your grade. Darryl Casey. Know him?"

"Oh. Casey. Sure," Matt said, thinking: *That airhead?*

"I actually played basketball myself," the detective said. "We lost to Rutland eight out of ten times, but we finally beat you my senior year. I saw your brother play. He was great. I know you've got a great family. People in Rutland think a lot of the Shaws. But, Matt, I have to tell you that I feel like these thefts were not an outside kind of thing. There was no evidence of breaking and entering, no signs of forced entry. I know some scary things can happen inside families, even in the really great families. I want you to know I can be your friend in this. In whatever's going on, if you're in trouble, or if you feel like someone else is in trouble, you can talk to me. Okay?"

Matt didn't say anything. He jammed his hands in his pockets, and kept on looking at the sidewalk.

"I also need you to know that I'm going to stick with this," she said. "It's my job. I need to find out what happened. I am going to do that." She said this softly, but in a firm way. "You don't have to talk to me now, but think about whether that might be a good idea, okay? I'm going to be asking more questions. There's been a series of crimes committed. But I also think someone may be in trouble here, in a personal kind of way. I want to do my job, but I also want to help. It's okay to trust me. Okay?"

He was still looking down; she stooped and looked up, trying to find his eyes. She found them. Matt nodded.

"Okay, well, that's all for now," she said. "But don't lose my card, all right? Don't put it through the wash or anything." She smiled that wide, freckly-faced smile. Matt reminded himself that she was a detective. If she could, she would put Neal in jail. If she could, she would tear his family to pieces.

"If you decide it's a good idea to share whatever it is that may be on your mind," she said, "give me a call. Any time—day or night. All right?"

Matt nodded. Then he stopped nodding.

"Okay then. Enjoy your day. I'll talk to you soon," she said, as if they were friends, and she turned to walk back to her car.

OLD STONES, NEW LEAVES

Matt turned the corner onto Grove Street and started walking the two long blocks to Stewart's. He wished he'd brought his iPod. In the morning he had left it on his dresser, knowing he was going to see Katie, looking forward to that and figuring he wouldn't need his music. It had felt kind of cool to leave the player behind, knowing something better would be happening. But now he felt different and needed his music. Now he was confused and didn't want to think about being confused.

He didn't want to think about a decent-seeming lady detective who said she'd keep asking questions, and also said he could trust her. How could he do that? He didn't want to trust her. But he also felt like something had to give, somewhere, somehow. Had to.

This was bad. He felt shaky and weak, like real trouble was coming now. He didn't want to think about it. He wanted his little bubble back, wanted the bass line loud in his headphones, wanted the beat that was strong behind the songs, his songs, that said something. He wanted to turn up Jai Quest and be in that space of righteousness and fortitude.

Jai Quest was his favorite artist because his rhymes were simple and strong, and Matt felt the truth inside them. So now Matt chose the songs he wanted from his memory and turned them up loud in his mind. His favorites lately were "Watch My Shadow" and "Truest Crime."

Yeah
Listen up now
Here I go

I'm a soldier
Lay your bets
One day older
Ain't dead yet
This is war
It's just me
Watch my shadow
Leave me be
I got no one
I can trust
Listen to me
While I bust it

Watch me go by, on my way
Gonna make it, it's my day
I'm a soldier, you don't know

What I'm feelin' never shows
Watch my shade
On the pavement
Gettin' paid
This ain't playin'
I got dreams
I will make it
Workin' schemes,
Never fakin'
You just watch me
Go my way
Fight this battle
Every day
I'm a soldier—lay your bets
One day older, ain't dead yet
Yeah

Let me say it
Yeah
Let me say
Yeah
This is war
It's just me
Watch my shadow
Leave me be

Yeah
That's right

Leave me be
You watch my shadow
You leave me be

Okay
Okay

Heard my girl
Heard my old girl
One I loved in high school
You know I been around the world
But back then we was like one
Just us two
She come back, asking friends
Sayin' that one was so real—
Say what happened to my man
Ask her girls
What's the deal

Girl he's gone
Blown away
He won't see another day
Just another tragedy
Just a memory on the street

Yeah
That was me

That was me
Here to tell you
That was me

Man I follow her so close
Could I just get one more dose
Of the love that we shared
Just one chance my soul to bear
But I can't call
Make no sound
Just a brother in the ground
Watch her walk places we'd go
See her cry, bendin' so low
I can't reach her I can't hold her
When I could, just one time,
Should a told her
Wish I'd told her
Man that was
My truest crime

Girl he's gone
Blown away
He won't see another day
Just another tragedy
Just a memory on the street

Yeah
Yeah

That was me
That was me
It was me, I do the time
All the time
For the truest crime
'Cause that was me
Yeah

· · ● · ·

As Katie watched Matt walk around the corner onto Grove Street, she didn't know what to think, what to do. What did Matt take from that woman? The bad thoughts she had been refusing to think, the gossipy speculations that other people had been making about Matt, now they were stacking up in her mind.

Was it drugs, after all? If it was, it had to be small—the white thing she had seen them pass was small. That would mean something hard, some terrible drug.

Or was it money? Was he selling for that woman? The woman hadn't looked like someone involved in stuff like that, but Katie had learned, living in her neighborhood, that people buying and selling dope didn't have to look like druggie people.

But wait, she thought. That might not be it at all. You really have no idea, she told herself. The car looked funny, too. Almost . . . official.

Katie pictured the car now: plain dark blue, with black tires and wheels and one long antenna.

Oh no. It was a police car, wasn't it?

Katie stood up. Matt was in trouble. He was! She knew, now, what she had seen: that lady was a plainclothes officer or detective, and she'd been waiting to talk to him on the street. And whatever it was about, Katie also knew he didn't deserve it. He didn't do it. Whatever they were thinking, it wasn't true.

Her mind was working fast now. All kinds of people had unfair and untrue theories about Matt; why couldn't the police have one, too? What did they know? And anyway, even if he had made a mistake, some kind of mistake, he was only a boy and boys make mistakes. They're built to make mistakes, right? They would hardly be boys, and they wouldn't need us, if they didn't. And he did need her. She knew he did. In just a minute he would get to Stewart's, and he had to find out that she would be there, too. He had to know that she would show up, that he could count on her.

Katie started half walking, half running down the street. She skittered to the corner, then dashed across to the far side of Grove Street. She could see him, walking up ahead; she wanted to yell to him, but didn't. She just walked fast and kept him locked in her sight. If he got to the store and turned around to look, he would see her. He would know she was coming.

· · ● · ·

There's a park up above and behind the back neighborhoods of Rutland where Katie and Matt had walked the day before. It's really just woods, this park—a shapeless, quiet preserve with a couple of ponds in there, well out of the way and unadvertised. You could live in the city for years and never know this park is there. Matt and Katie once again climbed into the hilly neighborhood of old homes, up a street that grew steadily more shadowed by trees among and behind the houses, till they came to a dead end.

A long metal pipe, a simple gate on a hinge, was padlocked chest-high across the place where the pavement stopped. Beyond that, a sign said this was a city park and forbade trespassing from midnight to six a.m. Behind that, just a wooded hill, slowly rising.

"Is this the right way in?" Katie asked.

Matt shrugged. "It's the way I come."

"I don't see any paths," she said, peering. "I sort of remember a path."

"Maybe that's the next street," Matt said. "I think you can go that way, too."

Katie was still peering. "Where do you go if there's no path?"

"Come on."

He led her over to a short, open knob, much smaller than a hill, at the front of the woods. Up the side of this knob ran a loose scar of orangey-brown dirt, a fresh cut torn open by some sort of use. Matt and Katie scrambled to the top of the knob. Up there was a single stunted pine tree, and some very old-looking gray rocks that were sunk most of the way in the ground, so that just the tops of them showed. The garish dirt cut continued across the top and down the other side.

Matt smiled. "Dirt bikes," he said.

"Oh."

"Kids. Boys. They go up, they go down. They go up, they go down." He grinned wider, and she actually, honest-to-god, felt her knees go weak. His eyes were a deeper blue than even the clear blue sky beyond his head. She wondered, looking into them, what was that color? He looked away but she was still wondering. Bluer than blue jeans when they were faded, she thought; but a clearer, less dense blue than new denim. She was trying to think if there wasn't some kind of glass, a bottled water or something, that was that amazing blue.

"Uh . . . so," Matt said. "I kind of just sit here, usually." He was looking down at a larger rock. It was old and mottled and it looked to her like the humped back of a small whale, slipping above the surface so the creature could breathe.

"Okay," she said. "Sure."

He sat down, and she sat beside him. It was a big enough rock that they didn't have to sit too close. It wasn't too awkward. Katie could feel some warmth coming through the old stone, which had soaked it up from the sunny spring day. They were looking out at a line of maple trees, a screen of trees that were tall and had their leaves just now emerging. Katie saw with happiness that all those fresh leaves were so new and so thin that the afternoon sun glowed softly right through them. The leaves looked like a host of tiny green lights, up high in each tree. Beyond them she could see backyards and houses, and in the distance the sunlit brick and steeples of the city. Beyond rose the old wooded mountains, a rumpled, high, and shadowy backdrop that just now was soft with the same new green.

Matt scratched in the ground with a stick. His head was bobbing just slightly. It had been bobbing slightly that way the whole time they'd been walking, as if he was listening to some music she couldn't hear. He had seemed glad to see her when she came hustling up to Stewart's; then he seemed in a hurry to walk down the busy street and get up into the quieter neighborhood. He had said almost nothing. So far Katie had asked nothing, even though she was desperate to know.

The questions, the wanting-to-know, pushed up from her chest against the tension in her throat. She felt she wasn't supposed to ask anything. But she couldn't say nothing.

"Matt?"

"Uh?"

"Ah . . . so . . ." She could feel her face grow warmer. She had no idea how to start.

"Is this, like, your favorite place, or no?"

"Oh, I don't know. Maybe not favorite. It's just one place I go."

"How come?"

"Well . . ." He scratched with the little stick at the soft layer of pine needles on the ground. "I don't know. There's nobody here, usually. I can just kind of sit."

"What about the boys and the bikes?"

"Sometimes they're here. Then I don't stay."

"Did you ride a lot? I mean, when you were younger?"

"Yeah! Sure. I loved my bike." He looked over. "You?"

"Yes. Oh yes! I still have it."

He nodded. "Me too." He smiled. "Sometimes we'd just

ride around in circles. Me and my friends. Just ride around and ride around."

"Yeah, us too. I remember," she said. This was some kind of opening. Some kind. He was talking. "You'd just keep moving," she said. "Even though you didn't really have anywhere to go."

He chuckled. "Yeah."

"We would talk and talk, me and my friends, all the time we rode around. Especially on summer nights. After dinner."

"Yeah." He nodded. "Us too."

"You kind of . . . you kind of walk around a lot now, huh?" she said.

He just kept scratching with that stick. "Yeah."

"Do you still feel kind of like you don't have anywhere to go?"

He shrugged. "I don't know."

She waited.

"Kind of, I guess," he said.

"And . . . maybe nobody to talk to," she said. They were both looking at the ground, not letting even their glances touch.

He shrugged again. No words this time.

She turned to him. "Matt. I'm not judging you," she said quickly. "You can talk to me. It'd be okay."

He didn't talk to her. He grabbed her and kissed her.

Katie was so startled, she froze; then she softened. His lips were sort of groping—moving, as if they were searching for the right place or the right hold. He turned his face and their noses collided, right in the bone place, and suddenly Katie's eyes were flooding.

She had to turn away. "Oh!" she said. "Oh, I'm . . ."

"God," he said. "Sorry."

"No." She turned back. "I'm not . . ." She was blinking to stop the tears, but that just made them spill down her face. His expression was like he'd just killed his own dog.

Suddenly she grinned. "My *God*," she said. "We are just totally pathetic, aren't we?"

He almost smiled, but his mouth was still wide and down-turned with horror. "Aaah," he said, shaking his head. "I guess."

"It's okay," she said. She wiped at her face. "It was an involuntary reaction."

"Uh . . . me too," he said. "Kind of. I mean I didn't totally mean to do that."

"No?"

"Well . . . I mean I guess I was thinking about it, ever since we sat down, or maybe sooner, but . . . anyway, I guess I really suck at it." He looked down. She felt a wave of tenderness for him. Such a confused boy.

"No," she said, moving closer, her eyes finally quiet. "No." He looked up and she kissed him. Now it was just warm and natural. They explored the warm, tender softness of each other's mouths. They turned gently now to be closer, and now his hand was on her back, holding her politely, it seemed, or uncertainly.

They kissed for a while, carefully. He didn't try to open his mouth or introduce his tongue. She was relieved. She didn't know how to do that.

Finally he drew away and looked at her. She went soft and closed her eyes, and he kissed her again. By instinct now. On the rock, his free hand moved to cover hers.

After a while they stopped kissing and were just looking at each other. His one hand stayed on her back, like it was stuck there. Then he dropped it and looked down.

"That was nice," Katie said. "We got better."

"Yeah."

But now, again, the desperate-to-know energy was pushing up at her throat.

"Matt," she said.

"Uh-huh?"

"That lady. I . . . I saw that lady. The one who was talking to you."

He didn't say anything. He didn't move. He was looking at the rock. She felt a seizure of tension, a spasm of it.

"I wasn't spying or anything," she said in a rush. "I saw you ahead of me, outside school, and I didn't know if I should try to catch up or if I should let you go ahead, 'cause you said you wanted to meet at Stewart's and you didn't say outside school, so I wasn't sure what to do and I was trying to decide, and then I saw you and I saw the lady get out of the car and I couldn't help it. I saw you talking. Or, I guess she was talking."

He nodded. Once.

"Matt." She leaned very close to his ear and spoke softly. "I want to be your friend."

Then he did something very strange. He let his face fall softly onto her shoulder. She was afraid he might cry, but he didn't. He didn't say or do anything. She sat there, almost paralyzed; then she wrapped her arms around him and held him. She was stroking his hair. She said, "It's okay," though she wasn't sure it was. He lifted his head. She thought he would talk but he started kissing her again. This time he did open his mouth, and she opened hers and he pushed her back, down, against the rock till she was lying there, and he was on top and they were kissing, and kissing, and open-mouthed kissing.

After a while things felt more unsure, more confusing, and then he lifted up and looked at her. She was gasping; he looked like he wasn't sure what to do.

"Whoa," she said, and sat up quickly. "Whoa." She was brushing her side and back, twisting to see what might be stuck to it.

"Are you okay?"

"Oh yes," she said.

Now they didn't, either of them, know what to do. They sat there side by side, holding hands and looking at the screen of trees, at all the light-cradling little leaves. At least, that's what she was looking at.

"I wonder what you think about," she said.

"Me? When?"

"When you walk around."

"Oh." He let go her hand, and with both of his he grabbed the crossed ankles of his legs. He started rocking slowly back and forth. She thought, *He's like some kind of hermit or some-*

thing. It's like he's got something inside him that he doesn't know what to do with, so he has to stay away. He has to keep it to himself.

He said, slowly, "I think . . . I don't know. I think about . . . God."

"You think about God?"

"No. I mean, maybe sometimes, but . . . I guess I think about whether anything means anything." He turned and looked at her. His eyes were searching now, and at once she knew what that blue was. It was the color you see in photographs of the earth from space. It was the blue of the ocean.

"I just don't know if . . . I mean, what difference does it make?"

She didn't know how to answer. She didn't understand the question. He looked down, picked up a sharp little pebble and scratched with it on the old mottled rock.

"I don't know," he said. "People just do stuff, the same stuff every day, over and over, 'cause they're supposed to or they're stuck doing it, or whatever, and in the end so what? I mean, in the end you're wiped out, you're wiped away, and what difference does any of it make?"

He was shaking his head, looking down. She studied the light-gray scratches he had made on the dark-gray rock.

"You can't know what difference you'll make," Katie said, slowly, carefully, "but you are part of something. We're all part of something. I think so. We all have things we're meant to do. People we're meant to care about. We're all meant to matter," she said.

He looked at her. "You believe that?"

She looked for humor or sarcasm in his eyes, but found none.

"Really. I do," she said. Now she looked down, a little embarrassed. "I don't feel like I have everything figured out, not at all. Mostly I have questions. But I do think . . . I mean, I do feel like we're all part of something. We're trying to figure out what that is. It's just hard sometimes."

She wrapped her arms around her bent legs, put her chin on her knee. She was afraid to look over at him.

"Hmm," he grunted. "But, like . . . how do you know it doesn't all just wash away? I mean, say you do something, or you try to help somebody or protect somebody or whatever. In a day or a week or a year, or after you're gone, how do you know if it makes any difference? At all?"

She sat there and looked, hugging her knees and thinking for a long time. Then she said, turning to him, "I brought something."

"To eat?"

"No." *God*, she thought: *boys*. Then she wished she could feed him. But she shook her head. "I brought some things. To show you."

"Okay."

She reached for her backpack, which lay on the pine needles. She zipped it open and reached way down, because what she had brought was heavy and had sunk to the bottom. She took out a purple felt bag, with a gold drawstring pulled tight at the top.

"Nice bag," he said.

"My mom gave me that." She pulled open the string, widened the mouth of the bag, reached in, and carefully, lovingly, began to bring out the things inside, to bring them out one at a time and place them on the pine needles.

TREASURES

First, out of the bag, she brought a shell. Just a regular gray seashell. She set it down very carefully, like it was a treasure. Then she brought out a small, smooth stone. It was flat and triangle-shaped, with rounded sides, and it was gray with spots of darker gray and streaks of pink. Unusual. It was almost shiny, too, like it had been polished.

Katie set that down beside the shell, and next drew out a long small stone that was purple and almost clear. He reached for that, and she put it in his palm. He held it up, putting his finger behind it. He could sort of see the finger through the smooth, light purple.

"This is quartz, right?"

"I'm not sure," she said, still sweetly intent on each new piece she was drawing out of the sack. Now it was a clear, longish, hard-edged rock, maybe four inches long. It looked like the Washington Monument, only see-through clear.

"This one I know is quartz," she said. "Quartz crystal."

"Cool." He reached for that and she traded it for the purple stone he'd been holding. She set the purple one down on the needles; then she drew out of the bag a flattish, very shiny oval stone that looked almost silver, then glossy black and then silver again as she turned it to show. She set that one down almost tenderly, even though, basically, it was a rock. Next she drew out a little stone that was pretty regular-looking except it was all white and glittery. Next was a cool little stone that looked like a layer cake, with thin strips of dark gray, sort of white, and then glittery purple on top, like piled-on icing. But, again, a rock.

Along with looking at the actual rocks, Matt also noticed the care with which she held each one in her fingertips. She would show it off at different angles for him, then each one she would set down as if that spot on the pine needles was a special place she had chosen just for that particular rock.

"So," he said, "are these, like, precious stones? Or something?"

She shrugged. She picked up the silver-black oval again, holding it up so they could both appreciate it. "This one I found on the beach," she said. "In New Hampshire. It was almost winter. We went for a day trip, my mom and me, when I was ten. We couldn't afford to stay over and it was cold anyway, but we walked on the beach and I found this." She set it down lovingly, then picked up the quartz Washington Monument.

"This one did come from a shop," she said. "My grandma Beth lives in Arizona now. She got it for me there. I have a littler one like it, too. They're quartz crystal."

126

"Yeah. You said."

"Uh-huh." She was holding it up to the light. "See: you can see through it." He squinted, his face right beside hers so their cheeks almost touched. He could see through just a center strip of the quartz; the rest was kind of clouded, or else light reflected off the sharp angles. But through the one strip, the central part, he could see through to the trees and their new green.

"Yeah," he said.

"Uh-huh." She set it down and Matt, looking at her, felt a pang shoot through him of urgent tenderness toward this pretty, bright-eyed, soft-haired girl and her purple bag of treasures that turned out to be rocks. Or rocks that turned out to be treasures.

She picked up the glittery purple layered one. It was really a nice purple, Matt thought. Funny that there were such colors, just in the ground.

"This I got when we had a fifth-grade trip to the Museum of Science in Boston," she said. "In that big gift shop. I used to know what the stone is called, but I forgot. My mom was a chaperone, and all I wanted to do was go to the gift shop. Isn't it nice?"

"Yeah," he said, looking at her face as she talked, at the way she smiled softly at the stone when she was telling its story.

She picked up a smooth, shiny, very black one he hadn't noticed before. "This one I found in the woods when I was little," she said. "When we lived in North Carolina, before we moved here, we had this friend, Saralynn Tracy. She was an older lady, and she really liked me. She used to take me into the woods and find stuff with me. She's the one who got me into finding rocks."

"Did it come this shiny?"

"No." She smiled, turning the smooth stone. At one end it had a pinched-in place, as if someone had rubbed a thumb into it for, oh, a thousand years. The whole stone was smooth as glass.

"Saralynn took it to a rock shop for me. They put it in a tumbler for like three days. It came out like this."

Now he reached for the shell. It was such a regular shell, that same kind that's on the sign for Shell gas—only this wasn't yellow, it was just a plain gray, lighter gray on its thin, delicate, converging ribs. At the bottom, where the ribs came together, one bit was broken off.

"What's special about this?" he said.

She colored. She took it from him with the tips of her fingers.

"I found that with my dad," she said very softly. "When I was little, before he left. Sometimes we'd go to the beach. I have this one, and a couple of others, left."

He took a breath and let it out.

"You probably miss him," he said. Lame.

She shrugged, set the shell on the needles. "I was pretty little."

"Yeah, but. He's still your dad."

She nodded. "Somewhere."

He wanted to touch her so badly, now, that he had no idea how to do it. No idea.

"Why rocks?" he said instead, and instantly thought that was *so* pathetic. But she brightened.

"Oh, I *love* rocks! When I was little I always had rocks in my pockets. I was always looking for them. I'd just pick them up. My mom used to keep a little pile of rocks by the washing machine that she picked out of my clothes. Whenever we'd go somewhere, anywhere I'd go, instead of bringing home a souvenir I'd bring home a rock. I don't really know why."

"So the smooth shiny ones came from those tumbler things?"

"Some of them." She nodded. "Some I got in shops, and they were tumbled. Other ones I found on the beach, or in streams. The water makes them smooth. Sometimes I'd get disappointed, though—I'd find something by the water that looked so shiny, 'cause it was wet. But then when I'd get it home and it would dry, it wouldn't look the same."

He just watched as she started picking up the stones one by one with her fingertips, and slipping them back into the purple bag. She stopped, holding one.

"I always pick them out by how they feel in my hand. I have to like how they feel. That's the most important thing, almost. Like this one. See?"

She handed him the smooth black one. The pinched end fit his thumb and forefinger perfectly.

"It's cool," he said. "Like it was made to hold."

"Isn't it? That's one of the reasons I like that one so much." She took it back, slipped it into the bag.

He said, "Can I see the bag?" She nodded and put it in his

hand. He could feel the shapes of the stones inside, and he heard seashells shifting in there with a soft clatter.

"At home I have a really nice box I keep my whole collection in," she said. "This is just my traveling bag."

He felt the heft of the bag on his palm.

"It's kind of like your voidcoat," he said.

She laughed. "Kind of! Whenever I feel really lonely, or sad, I take it out and spread everything out on my bedspread. I remember about each one."

"You always remember their story? Where you got them?"

"Oh, yes. That's why I have them."

"Hmm." He was just looking at the bag again. "It's cool that they're not precious gems or anything. They're just basically rocks. And shells," he added quickly.

She leaned over suddenly so that her face was close. He thought she might kiss him. He wanted her to.

"I didn't bring these for any big reason—I just wanted to show you," Katie said. "But, I mean, you're right. They are just rocks. But they mean something."

"Well, yeah, but . . ." He put the bag down. "They only mean something because you think they mean something. Otherwise, I mean they're nice, but they're just rocks."

"Well, okay. Sure. But if rocks can mean something because I think they mean something, why can't you mean something if *you* think you mean something?"

He thought. He thought some more. Finally he said, "Huh?"

"I mean you can decide things are meaningless, or you can

decide things are meaningful," she said. "It's up to you. It's a *choice*."

"So it's all in our minds? It's all empty unless we have some kind of illusion?"

"Sheesh—you *do* need the voidcoat," she said, smiling into his eyes until she saw how searchingly he was looking into hers.

"Well . . . my rocks aren't illusions," she said. She slapped the warm stone they sat on: "*This* rock isn't an illusion. You're not an illusion either. Neither is anything you see, unless you're crazy, which I don't think you are, though I'm not sure you should keep going in this direction. But the thing is, if you care, things matter. If you don't, they're just things. That doesn't mean they're meaningless—they're still *here*."

She paused, searching for what she was talking about.

"Maybe everything means something," she said finally, slowly, puzzling it out. "Maybe we only see that about the things and people we care about—but maybe that's just us. You know?"

He shook his head. "No."

"Okay. Here," she said, plunging her hand back into the purple bag and fishing around. She knew by years of feel the one she wanted. She drew it out.

It was the smooth black stone again.

"This is the one I got with Saralynn. When we took it to the rock shop, the people there said it's a kind of rock that's supposed to protect you."

"Protect you?"

"Yes. From evil and stuff. So it's special. But I could just throw it away." She fisted it and cocked her arm suddenly; he grabbed her fist.

"Don't! God."

"But I *could*," she said. "Then it would be out there in the woods. We could look for hours. We'd probably never find it, but it would still matter to me. I would still remember it. But maybe . . . maybe if I really understood, if I really *knew*, then all the rocks and pebbles and leaves and pieces of dirt out there would all matter. Everything would. Also all the people—not just the ones I know. You know? Maybe I only see the importance in a few things because of my limitations. Maybe the fewer limits I have, the more I know how much everything means, really."

He shrugged. "Or maybe the more you know how people really are, what people can really do, the less anything means anything."

She looked at him a long time.

"You don't mean that," she said. "Not really."

"I don't *want* to. But people really let you down sometimes, you know?"

"They sell their soul," she said, very softly and riskily, repeating what he had written once.

He looked down. "Yeah."

"But maybe *they* don't see," she said. "Maybe you still can—and if you still do, maybe they can again someday. You know?"

He was looking into her eyes, and she kissed him, very softly and warmly. There was no touching or awkwardness this time; they just kissed, breathing together. Then she separated from him, and looked down at their finger-twined hands. She loosened hers from his, then with her fingers she opened his hand. She placed the black stone on his palm. She closed his hand on her most potent treasure.

"Now it's yours."

"No! No way."

"I want you to have it. I really do. I think you need it."

He held it. He felt it, in there.

"See?" she said. "It matters."

"I like you," he said.

"I like you, too." She waited. "A lot," she said.

At first he didn't answer. She waited again, her heart teetering.

"I like you a lot, too," he said.

They kissed again, just kissing, for a while. Neither knew how long. There was just the warmness of their lips together, and their tongues sometimes touching, trying places, almost like talking. Finally she drew apart and said, "Umm . . . I think I might have to get home. If my mom comes home from work and I'm not there, I have to provide a detailed explanation."

He stood up. "We might want to avoid that," he said.

"It would be wise," she said, taking his hand. They started down the dirt-bike scar, past the metal gate, back toward town.

• • ● • •

They did not talk until they came down the neighborhood to where they could see the correctional center.

"There was a robbery," Matt said.

"What?"

"A robbery."

"There was? Where?"

"At my house." It was like he was eking out the words.

"Oh God," Katie said.

"That's why she talked to me."

"Who?"

"That lady. The one you saw."

"Oh. Yes?"

"Yeah. She's a detective."

"Ohhh," Katie said. "I wondered. About that car."

"An unmarked car."

"Yes. They might as well hang a sign on it."

"I didn't do it," Matt said.

"You didn't hang a sign on it?"

"No. The burglary. It wasn't me."

Katie squeezed his hand. "I know."

They walked for a while, past the high brick walls of the jail. They were coming up State Street; they could see the low brick Stewart's store now.

"Does she have any clues?" Katie asked.

"I'm not sure. She gave me her card." Matt fished in his jeans and pulled it out. Katie felt a wave of pure relief.

"Carolyn Casey," she read. "A lady detective. Wow."

Matt nodded. "She looked pretty young. And stuff."

"Hmm."

"She wants me to trust her. To talk to her, you know? But I don't know what she thinks."

"Maybe she's not sure either," Katie said. "Do you want to talk to her?"

Matt just looked at the ground as they walked.

"There were three robberies," he said.

"Three?"

"Yeah."

"Did you know?"

"No. First my mom was missing something, some jewelry. Then my dad. A watch, I think. Finally it was my dad's stereo amp. That one everybody noticed. That's when they called it in."

They walked. Then Katie said, very carefully, "Do you have any clues?"

She looked at him. Matt just shrugged. His mouth was a thin line, the muscles tight around it. She squeezed his hand.

"It's okay," she said. "Isn't it?"

But he shook his head.

IN THE FLOW

When he woke up on Saturday morning, Matt didn't worry about Neal, he didn't worry about coming downstairs, he didn't worry about seeing his mom or his dad or what they would say. He didn't think about those things at all.

His mom, who gave him toaster waffles for breakfast, was looking at him again with those woeful, baffled eyes, but Matt barely noticed. As he ate he kept remembering Katie's face, just as he had kept on seeing it, in his mind, all the night before until he had finally fallen asleep. He remembered Katie's face as she came up to the Stewart's, walking fast, looking worried. Katie's face when they'd bashed noses and her eyes were watering and she was so embarrassed. Katie's face as she looked soft-eyed at her treasures, as she set them down on the pine needles.

"What are you going to do today?" his mom asked.

"Huh?"

She sat down quickly, as if Matt's distracted grunt was the opening she'd been hoping for.

"I just realize I'm not paying enough attention to what you're doing," his mom said, and suddenly her eyes filled with tears. "I feel like I've failed you," she said, placing her hand on his arm. "I feel like it's my fault."

"What? Mom, I haven't done anything."

"Matthew, you can talk to me. You can. I know we haven't talked enough lately. You boys have always been so great about taking care of each other. But I'm feeling so afraid you've gotten somewhere that even your brother can't help. Oh Matt . . . I'm *so* sorry I haven't been there for you."

She was crying now. He just stared at her, not believing this.

"Mom . . ."

"I'm sorry. I'm *sorry*." She reached for a tissue. "I just want you to know that I won't judge you. I'm your *mom*. I'm on your side. You can . . ." She blew her nose honkingly. "You can talk to me."

Matt thought, *And what would you say? If you really knew?*

"Okay, Mom. But . . . I didn't take that stuff. Any of it. Honestly. I would never do that."

"Then where do you *go*?" She honked her nose again. "Where are you going right now?"

"Over to KJ's. To shoot hoops."

"To shoot?" Her eyes filled up again. "Oh, Matthew, to hear you talk about shooting again . . . that's so *wonderful*."

He felt his skin crawl. He got up, nodded at her, and left.

$$\cdot \; \cdot \; \bullet \; \cdot \; \cdot$$

Katie was back in his mind before he got out the door. It wasn't so much that he was thinking about her, unless "she likes me, she likes me, she *really likes* me" is thinking. It was more that he felt lifted up. Holding that thought, "she likes me," remembering how she looked, remembering her saying "I like you . . . a lot"—these things kept him up here in the feeling. Up here in the feeling was the only place he wanted to be, and he stayed in the feeling as he walked across the side yard to KJ's.

He had seen KJ in his driveway practicing, and was glad he was still there. KJ was doing a spin move to a layup, then taking the ball again as it dropped through, when he saw Matt coming. He stopped dead for only a second. Then he nodded once, dribbled out, and took a turnaround jumper.

The ball angled off the back rim toward Matt, who stepped onto the driveway court and caught it on the bounce. He dribbled toward KJ, shoulder-feinted and lifted up a jumper. It banged off the front rim. KJ just turned and watched as Matt took off after the rebound and grabbed it before it bounced onto the grass.

Matt glided in from the side for a layup, got the ball back, dribbled it out, shot again, missed, loped after it, caught it and dribbled once, then squared to the basket, his knees bending. He rose up straight and spun the ball off his fingertips. It swished.

"Dude," KJ said. He went for the ball and, respecting playground etiquette, fed it back. Matt caught it, rose in rhythm, and scored. KJ fed and he swished it again. Matt moved sideways as KJ retrieved and fed; he shot again, missed, got the bounce, and went up in one smooth motion. KJ watched it kiss the back of the net as it slipped through.

They shot around without a word for ten minutes at least. Matt felt the rhythm again, felt like Katie was with him and he was in the flow. He wanted her to be watching. He wanted her there really. When he started thinking about that, his shots started clanking off the rim; so then it was KJ's turn and Matt quietly moved in to feed him the ball. KJ made a couple, and when he missed one Matt fed him again anyway. They didn't have to say anything. They had been doing this since second grade.

After a while, KJ brightened even more.

"Dude," he said as he hefted the ball, spun it between his fingers, and lofted a shot. He fell backward as he let it go.

"Don't fall back," Matt said. "Go up straight."

The ball bounced off the front rim.

"See?" Matt said, catching it. "Fall back and you'll be short."

"Yeah, okay," KJ said. "But did you hear about Gutterson's lawn mower?"

"Gutterson's *lawn* mower? Why?" Paul Gutterson lived nearby, in a dead end off Grove Street.

"Their lawn mower died," KJ said. "It's old—a 1972 John Deere Model 70 lawn tractor. I know this 'cause Gutterson said so. His dad said he could have it, he can do what he wants with it. His dad's getting a new one."

The feeling about Katie was singing loud inside Matt. It felt great to have that and keep it private inside him.

"Why do we care?" Matt said. He was having fun.

"Be*cause*, Gutterson and Fornaccio are turning it into an on-road/off-road racing machine." KJ cradled his ball. "Dude, you have to see this. They are tricking it out totally. They're putting in a motorcycle engine, with a big-bore kit like the dirt bikes use, and an air intake. With a scoop."

"A scoop?"

"A scoop. And they're lightening the whole deck. You know the lawn mower deck, where the blade's underneath? They're replacing all the deck parts with lighter metal, and a titanium blade, and they're gonna widen the wheel base for cornering . . ."

"Wait a minute. They're putting in a titanium blade?"

"Yeah."

"A *lawn* mower blade?"

KJ grinned delightedly. "Yeah! They say it'll be able to do sixty."

"On the *lawn*?"

"No—on-road. Off-road, maybe forty-five. They're putting on new tires, new rims, new clutch, new pistons, and, of course, new headers, got to have the headers . . ."

"Oh yes," Matt said. "Absolutely. Headers."

"And a new throttle control pedal, so they can run at different speeds—you know a rider mower's usually got just the one speed—and they're repainting it, too. The traditional green, with yellow trim. And lots of chrome."

KJ grinned hugely. "Isn't that the wildest thing you ever heard?"

"Are they actually doing any of this, or are they just talking about it?"

"They're doing it! Want to go see?"

Katie had said she couldn't do anything till later today, that Saturday was cleaning day at home. They could talk later, she'd said, and maybe they could meet. So Matt had these hours to fill.

"Well . . . sure," he said. "Yeah."

They took off across the lawn. KJ was still cradling his ball.

· · ● · ·

Katie barely heard the phone through the high whining of the vacuum cleaner she was pushing. But she did hear it, like an alarm clock insisting itself into a really noisy dream. She thought it might be Matt so she dropped the vacuum hose, left the machine running, and dashed for the phone before her mom could get there first.

"Hello?"

"Hi, Coots."

Oh. It was Hope. Only Hope called her that. In fifth grade there had been a long spasm of obsession with cooties, mainly among boys, of course. Katie had responded by earnestly asking absolutely everyone if they could explain to her what a cootie actually was. No one could, but afterward, when it was just the two of them, Hope had started calling her Cootie, which had since become Coots.

"Hi, Hoop," Katie said, sounding disappointed.

"Hmmm," said Hope. "Hoping for someone different?"

"Well . . . maybe."

"Coots, my God, what's that shrieking? Did you finally drive Darcy insane?"

"No, no, she's cleaning the bathroom," Katie said of her mom. "That's the vacuum."

"Oh right. It's *cleaning* day."

"I could turn it off."

"I would."

"Right."

At last the vacuum wheezed down to silence.

"I'm back," Katie said.

"So. *Tell* me."

Katie didn't answer.

"Coots?"

"Yes?"

"Tell me about it?"

Again, silence.

"Something's wrong, isn't it?" said Hope.

"No. Oh no. I just . . . I'm not sure what to tell."

"Have you seen him?"

"Yes."

"Do you like him? Still?"

"Yes."

"More?"

"Yes."

"A lot more?"

"Yes."

"A really whole lot more?"

Another pause. "Yes."

"O . . . kay. A whole lot should I be worried more?"

"Why should you be worried?" Katie said quickly.

"Well . . . I don't know. I was just wondering."

"Why should you be wondering?"

"Whoa, Katie, don't get defensive. It's me."

"I'm not defensive. I just . . . No matter what I say, you'll be worried, right? Because it's him."

"No. That's not true."

"It is true. It's like 'worried' is a code word. You all think there's something wrong with him. Something weird or, like, criminal about him."

"No, we don't."

"Yes you do. I know you do. But you don't know him. You don't know anything actual to worry about. So you just assume."

"You sound so different," Hope said softly. "I could worry about that."

"I'm not different," Katie said. "*It's* different."

"What is?"

"Us."

"Us four? We're different?"

"No," Katie said impatiently. "Him and me. Us."

There was a long silence.

"What?" Katie said.

"I didn't say anything."

"I know. But what?"

"Katie . . . how come you won't talk to anybody about this?"

"I don't know. It's just kind of personal, I guess."

"Katie, we're your best friends. Personal stuff is what we *talk* about. We always have. Right?"

Katie felt guilty, sad, and defensive all at once.

"I don't know what to say," she said.

"Well? Does he like you?"

"Yes."

"Did he tell you?"

"Oh yes."

"What did he say?"

"He just said he likes me. A lot, actually."

"He said a lot?"

"Yes. And anyway I knew."

"How?"

"He just . . . showed me. We showed each other."

"Katie. You didn't."

"I didn't *what*?"

"You know."

"No. I don't know. Hope, why can't you just trust me? Can't anybody just trust me, ever? Why do you have to find some big *drama* in this?"

There was a pause.

"Should I start with question A, B, or C?" Hope asked.

"What?"

"Sorry. A joke. Anyway I'm not trying to find drama. I'm just trying to talk to you."

"No, you're trying to make drama. Now you want to know if he *raped* me."

"Katie!"

"What?"

Katie heard the catch in Hope's breathing and knew she had gone too far.

"I'm sorry, Hoops. I'm sorry." Katie started to tear up, too.

"I know." Katie heard Hope snuffle, just once.

"I would really really like to just be happy for you," Hope said. "It's just that . . . you seem so *different* all of a sudden. I don't know. Something doesn't feel right about it. You know?"

"But it's good. It's good for me. It really is. It couldn't be just us forever, Hope," she said, and instantly wished she hadn't.

Usually at this point in a conversation Hope would come up with something clever and slightly darkly humorous that would sum everything up, or would at least make you laugh. But instead she said, in a quiet voice, "We're still your best friends, Katie. Even if you don't think you need us anymore."

Katie was horrified and started to answer, but the phone went dead. She stood looking at it, feeling like some slimy creature that should be hiding under a rock. Then she was angry and defensive, and she wondered *why?* Why did that just happen? And then she wondered if there really *was* something going on that wasn't right, that didn't feel right. Or did her friends just not want to be left out? Was it so terrible that she really liked somebody and that he liked her? What was so wrong-feeling about that?

Then from the bathroom her mother said, "Katie, are you done in there already?"

· · ● · ·

Somehow, Paul Gutterson's dad had convinced his mom to let the boys and the old John Deere Model 70 have one whole bay of the family's two-car garage. The radio was playing, outside it was a softly sunny spring Saturday, and in here Gutterson and his best friend David Fornaccio were surrounded by disman-tled lawn mower parts. They had black grease up their arms and horsepower dreams in their eyes.

"*Titanium blade*," Gutterson said.

"Where does a person *get* a titanium lawn mower blade?" Matt asked.

"You can get all this stuff easy," Fornaccio said, pausing from turning a ratchet wrench on the wide deck that protected the blade. "There's whole Web sites on tricking out lawn mow-ers."

Matt just shook his head, and from then on he watched. He wasn't mechanical at all; he was in the flow again, in the flow of having spent time shooting the ball again, and in the flow of something so much deeper and more exciting than that. He just watched the guys work, and he half heard KJ's many questions about what was what. The boys really did seem to know the parts, and their plans, too. Matt one-quarter listened and three-quarters stayed up inside the singing in his mind.

At one point Fornaccio, who was very mechanical and always said exactly what was on his mind, set the wrench down and peered at Matt.

"Man," Fornaccio said, shaking his head, "whatever you took this morning, I want some."

"What?"

"You look like you're on drugs, man—really nice drugs. Hey, is that it? They finally get you on some of those anti-depressants? So you'd have this little *smile* all the time and you wouldn't be so weird anymore?"

Matt could have said something like "Bite me, Fornaccio"—that would have been the thing for a ninth-grade boy to say, in this situation—but he didn't. He just smiled and waited, cocooned in his secret feeling, for the guys to stop looking at him, to go back to their parts and plans and mechanical excitement, which was so totally different from his.

· • ● • ·

When the phone rang again, Katie was scrubbing the sink. Not surprisingly, it was Sam.

"Katie. What did you say to Hope?"

"Why?"

"Well, she's totally traumatized."

"Well . . . she is?"

"Yes. She called Tamra and Tamra called me. She said she doesn't understand what's really going on, but you won't talk to her."

"Who said that? Tamra?"

"No, Hope. She told Tamra and Tamra told me."

"But . . . I did talk to her."

"Does he really like you?" Sam said, her voice eager now.

"Yes."

"Is he going to call you?"

"I don't know. Not right now. I told him I was cleaning. Which I am, by the way."

"Did you do anything?"

"No, Sam. Well . . . a little."

"What?"

"We just kissed."

"Just a little?"

"Well . . . more than a little."

"Oooh. How is he?"

Actually, in part Katie loved these questions. She wanted to tell everything. But she felt disloyal or something, even thinking about exposing what was private with him. She knew he wouldn't want that. So her answers came out almost grouchy.

"He's fine, Sam. He's good."

"Does he want to see you again?"

"Yes. Later."

"Tonight?"

"Yes, Sam."

"You have to tell us everything."

"No I don't. I'm not going to."

A pause. "Why not?"

"Because it's private."

"It's what?"

"It's *private*, Sam. Because you would get on the phone and tell those two and then you'd IM everyone you know, and then you'd start telling people you *don't* know."

"Sheesh," Sam said. "For someone who's supposed to be in love you're sure edgy."

For a second, those words "in love" rang in Katie like a church bell. Then she took a breath.

"I just . . . I need to keep this private between us," she said.

"Between you and me?"

"Between him and me."

"Why?"

"It's just really early and really incredible and, I don't know . . . it feels like it needs to be private right now."

"It's incredible?"

"What?"

"You said it's incredible."

"And I said it's private."

"But why? Are you like in his secrecy now?"

"*No,*" Katie said sharply. "Will everybody please quit it with the drama?"

"With the what?"

"With the *drama*. If it's not sex it's secrecy. Everybody's got to whip up something ridiculous about this."

After a second Sam said, "I really don't understand what you're talking about."

Katie was breathing hard. "Sam . . . I just want it to be him and me. We need it to be just us. For now. Is that so strange?"

"I don't know. I guess not. But . . . I just don't get why you're so edgy when you're supposed to be happy. And why you're so private when you're supposed to be sharing with your *best friends.*"

"I'm supposed to be cleaning," Katie said, now pretty successfully fighting off the guilt of disappointing her friends. "I have to go now, Sam. I really have to clean."

"Well, okay . . ."

Katie hung up feeling totally exhausted by people's questions. Why did people have to have so many *questions*?

· · ● · ·

When they got bored with the lawn mower boys, Matt and KJ ambled back to KJ's driveway. KJ still cradled the ball like he was carrying a baby, except that when he could, he bounced it.

"I want to paint the lines," KJ said when they had reached his driveway and were standing at its edge, on the greening grass.

"The what?"

"The lines, man. You know, the foul line, the key and everything. I want to paint it. Like a court. Even the three-point line. There's room; I measured."

"Huh."

"Then when I step on, it'll be like a real court. Between the lines, all business. Just like MJ." He stepped onto the asphalt, dribbled, and lifted up a three-pointer. It swished.

"Dude," he said, turning back to Matt.

Matt grinned and nodded, and they bumped fists. KJ, excited, said, "I've been working on MJ's fadeaway. You know? Nobody could *ever* block it."

"Yeah, but . . ."

"Check this out," KJ said. He started dribbling busily, his back to the basket. Now he spun to face the bucket, and jumped—not just up, but more backward. He barely got the shot off. It missed everything.

"Okay, it needs work," he said, grinning.

"It doesn't need work, it's *wrong*," Matt said. KJ looked at him, puzzled, and Matt said, "Okay, look. Michael Jordan had incredible spring and body control, and he could do that, right? But for you and me, for regular people, it's the wrong way to shoot, falling back. It throws your trajectory off."

"You could do it," KJ said.

"No, man—I wouldn't try. You have to play *solid*. That's the first thing—you have to do it right in the basic ways. Then maybe if you improve to that level you can improvise and add your style, but first you have to do it *right*. You square up to the basket and you go up straight. Every time. Lift it straight over your head and spin it straight off your fingers. Then the shot's true. You know where it's going. If you go falling back to be fancy, you're out of control, and your shot won't be the same every time. Then it doesn't matter if nobody can block it, 'cause even if it goes in, it's only by accident. See?"

"Show."

"Okay." Matt dribbled, his back to the bucket. He spun and stopped, knees bent. "See? Both feet pointing right at the basket. Body square to it. See?"

KJ nodded.

Matt went up, drew the ball overhead, spun it off his fingertips. It slipped through the net.

KJ nodded.

"It's *simple*," said Matt. "You know this."

"Yeah." KJ was looking down.

"What?"

KJ shrugged. Finally he said, "I wish I had what you have."

"But . . . hey, everybody's different, right? If you play a fundamental game, if you practice it straight up so it's the basis of everything you do, then you can be solid in your own way. On whatever level you play. It doesn't matter, see? It's the feeling of doing it solid that matters. Doing it good."

KJ brightened. "I like that."

"Yeah," said Matt. "Yeah. Me too."

They spent the afternoon shooting and reminiscing, then lying on the grass and reminiscing some more. KJ knew not to ask Matt about the present, about what was going on that he would not talk about—so they talked about the past. Along with basketball they'd played flag football in the city league, and Midget League and Little League and Babe Ruth baseball together, sometimes on the same team, sometimes against each other, so there was lots to remember. Matt enjoyed it. At the same time, all through the afternoon he kept a big part of his mind lit up with what was really on it. It was like there was a bright, secret sunroom with just him and Katie in it.

"Dude," said KJ, "Okay, remember the West Rutland holiday tournament? Fifth grade? The finals?"

"Yeah," Matt said. It didn't take much effort. If he wanted to see her face in his mind, there she was. Right there.

"Remember? We'd just scored and we were down one with like fifteen seconds left. To Castleton," KJ said.

"I thought it was Christ the King," Matt said vaguely. He liked how her hair swung and bounced, brown and shiny, when she walked alongside him.

"No, it was Castleton. They got the in-bounds in, and that kid Morrissey had it. The one who thought he was so hot. Remember him?"

"Uh-huh." He could see her brown eyes light up when she liked something he'd said. He liked the way she smiled. "He moved away somewhere," Matt said.

"Yeah, but that was the next year," KJ said. "You remember, though? He started to bring it up. You were on him, and he was looking at you."

"You came up on his blind side," Matt said, remembering again how she placed those rocks down on the pine needles. And then how she closed her eyes and tilted her head, just before she kissed him.

"Yeah, and I tapped it loose," KJ said. "You grabbed it, and

I went for the bucket. You passed it to me right over that Morrissey kid's head. Remember?"

Matt just nodded. He could smell her. He closed his eyes.

"Yeah," KJ said. "And I got it on the run. Layup, buzzer, trophy."

It was one of KJ's favorite memories. They'd made the play together, but for once it had been KJ making the big bucket. Matt nodded, his eyes still closed, remembering something KJ didn't know about. And every once in a while he secretly slipped his hand into the cargo pocket of his shorts, where he kept Katie's shiny black protective stone.

TRADE

Katie wanted to leave—she wanted to call Matt and go meet up with him—but her mom felt they weren't done cleaning yet. Katie felt they were, they absolutely were done right now, and the two of them wound up having a furious fight over, as usual, basically nothing. Katie got grounded for the night. For Saturday night, which made her even more furious. So after a silent siege of a dinner, Katie, who never broke rules of any kind, went to her room, shut the door tight, and called Matt.

"I'm grounded," she said. "Can you come over?"

They agreed that Matt would come sneak into her backyard, through the dark side yard. Katie would wait till her mom was in the living room with her friend Ellie from the Price Chopper, watching the video they'd rented from work. It was some love story. Katie knew that meant her mom would be totally absorbed for a good hour and a half. She slipped out the kitchen door and down the back steps.

They kissed and they whispered. And they kissed. Matt brushed her breasts a few times, as if by accident, and she felt thrilled and also nervous about that. But mainly he just seemed to want to kiss her and look at her. She loved the way he looked at her now.

"Can we go over to your house sometime?" she whispered. The moon was up, and its light bathed the backyard. The tree and the clothesline cast shadows on the silvery grass. It gave her shivers.

He shook his head.

"No?" she whispered.

He shook his head again.

"Why not?"

"It's just not cool."

She wanted to ask why not again, but she knew she had stepped in the area of stuff she shouldn't ask about. So she didn't. She wondered why it wasn't cool, but made herself stop wondering. She just said, "Where will we go, then?"

He shrugged. "Here?"

Katie shook her head. "When my mom's not home she has the downstairs neighbor, Mrs. Prescott, watch to make sure nobody but me comes in or out. My mom's obsessed with making sure some guy doesn't impregnate me and ruin my life so that I wind up at the register next to hers at the Price Chopper."

Matt looked at her very seriously. "You can't ruin your life. You're so . . . smart. You've got to have a really incredible life."

"Yes, but *my* life. She's scared I'll mess up the way she did. Why would I do that?"

Matt was looking at her that way again. "Your mom didn't mess up," he said. "She had you."

Katie felt herself filling from bottom to top, so that she had to kiss him again.

· · ● · ·

Later in the evening, Matt made the longish walk home on a carpet of air. Once again he hadn't brought his iPod. He almost didn't want his music right now; his songs didn't fit. The whole way home, in fact, he kept remembering this one old song— this was so sappy he was embarrassed to be thinking about it, but he kept remembering that "Over the Rainbow" song. From *The Wizard of Oz*. He couldn't bring up too many of the words, but he did remember that part about troubles melting like, what was it? Lemon drops? He liked lemon drops.

When he got all the way to his own neighborhood and started to walk past the houses out there, he liked seeing their lights on, yellow and warm. He liked the yellow streetlights, too. Even the headlights of the passing cars. The air was warm and alive, and so was he.

Matt trotted up his driveway, buzzing with the idea that he would get right online and write something to Katie, something short but nice, and then he'd find that "Over the Rainbow" song. It was silly but he wanted it. He wouldn't need to tell anyone, though maybe he would tell Katie. Hurrying around back of the house, he saw another loser's beat-up car parked there, outside the garage with its lights on and its engine running.

Someone was sitting in the driver's seat. The patio door to Neal's room was open, like maybe Neal was just coming out or had just gone back in, or something. Neal had had his own car, an old blue Corolla, but a few weeks ago he'd suddenly sold it. That was a week or so before he'd started stealing stuff. The money from the car seemed not to have lasted long.

Matt was thinking that after he'd downloaded the song, he might listen to it and write down some of the lyrics, like that part about dreams coming true, so he could send them to Katie. Or he could just download the words from a lyrics site. That would be quicker; he could send them to her sooner. Maybe she would sing the song in her mind, too, like he was right now. He was wondering if she would call him right away to tell him how much she liked it. He imagined what she would say while he bounded up the stairs of his house, which was empty as usual, his parents off somewhere. Then he opened his bedroom door and saw that the iPod he had left on his dresser was gone.

Matt hadn't moved so fast in months. He was downstairs, through the kitchen, and out the back door in time to see Neal bending into the passenger seat of the loser friend's car. Matt yelled *"Hey!"* and Neal's head popped up, above the car's roof. Then it ducked back down and the door slammed. In about two seconds Matt was in front of the car. The car gave a little burp and popped forward; Matt stood there. The driver stopped and Matt slammed both hands on the hood. He stayed right there, glaring.

Now it looked like the two dark shapes of the guys inside the car were arguing. Their hands flared, pointing in Matt's direction. Then the loser friend in the driver's seat shook his head. It looked almost like Neal had said "*Go*, man, just go, *make* him move," and the friend had said something like "No way. No freaking way." Neal's shape lunged over and pounded the horn. Matt flinched a second, but he held his ground and kept on glaring.

The passenger door jerked open to the sound of cursing. Neal lunged out and came around toward him.

"What are you *doing*? Are you *crazy*?" Neal's voice was screechy. His eyes were bulging.

"I can't believe you did this," Matt said. "To *me*."

"Did what? Will you *move*?"

Neal, four inches taller but skinny now, shoved him. Matt held his ground. Neal drew back and lunged to shove him again, but as he came forward Matt caught his brother's hands and gripped them hard. Neal's head and shoulders were working back and forth; his eyes were darting all over.

"You asshole, you loser, let me *go!*" Neal said. "Will you let me *go*?"

"Neal," Matt said. "*Neal*. You stole from *me*."

"I did *not*. Will you let . . ."

"From *me*, Neal. I bet it's right . . ." Matt saw something square-edged outlined by the headlights in the cargo pocket of Neal's pants. He let go one wrist and slapped at the pocket. He felt something hard and rectangular in there as Neal jumped backward.

"*Let me go!*" Neal swung at Matt's face with his free hand, but he was shaky and Matt caught his wrist again. Neal, captured, roared into a rage.

"I will *freaking kill you*, you little *shit*! You have *no idea* what you're dealing with!" Neal was shrieking in Matt's face now; he had white stuff around the edges of his mouth, dried spit or something. His eyes were wild, shooting out sharp rays of desperation.

"You get out of the way *now*, you loser piece of shit, you let me go *now*—'cause I *will* kill you, all right? We will run you the fuck over, all *right*? I don't have any and I have to get some, it's gonna *happen*, I don't care what I have to do to you, this is *going to happen*, all *right*?"

"Neal . . ."

"I didn't take *anything*! I didn't! You little piece of shit, *let me go*! It doesn't matter anyway, you'll get it back, but right now I have to *get* something. Right *now*!"

"Not with my iPod, you don't," Matt said evenly. "No way, Neal. Figure out something else."

Neal seemed to be trying to focus, to slow down. He settled his breathing some, but there was still that hyper, glaring energy in his eyes.

"I did!" he said. "I did! I have something new. It's gonna happen—it's just getting started. This doesn't ever have to happen again, it won't ever happen again. But *now* I got to go. *Now*. You don't understand. You *don't understand anything*. Right *now* I have to go and do this."

"No. Give it back."

"I don't have anything! Man, *I have to do this*!" Neal was in his face now, lying and pleading and panicking all at once. Matt still held his wrists and they were jerking back and forth, as if the brothers were two boys wrestling over a toy. Neal twisted one arm and with a violent jerk he yanked it free, then swung it overhand and smashed Matt on the ear.

"Ow! Jesus!" Matt's hand went to his ear and Neal broke away, danced back out of reach, and darted for the car. He leaped in and locked the door. Matt pounded both fists on the hood, still blocking the way. He could see the dark shapes inside arguing again.

Neal rolled his window down an inch.

"You have money. Right?" he said.

"What?"

"You have *money*. Right?"

"Why? Neal, what the . . ."

"Forty bucks. Get me forty bucks."

"For what?"

"For your thing."

"I thought you didn't have it."

"What I have to *have* is forty bucks. Bring it now or we take off. We will *run you over*. That's *it*. I'm *done* with this shit."

Matt thought. "Jesus, Neal . . . I don't have forty bucks."

"How much then?"

"I don't know . . . maybe thirty, thirty-five, thirty-seven . . ."

"That'll work. Get it and you can have your thing back."

"What?"

"Get it. That's it. Just *get* it."

"Neal . . . I'm supposed to go upstairs and trust you to stay here? Trust *you*?"

"All right. Whatever. I'll come." Neal opened the passenger door a crack. Matt stepped back.

"You go first," Matt said.

What had become a completely surreal experience now had Matt stalking behind his own brother as Neal hurried through the kitchen and up the stairs. Neal stopped at Matt's door, which Matt in his earlier good feeling had left unlocked. Neal turned the knob, shoved the door open, and stepped right in.

Matt sidled in behind. He eyed his brother warily. If Neal made a move to run, Matt was set to spring at him and jam him into the doorframe. Neal didn't run. He watched Matt like a predator, rigid with tension, only his eyes moving.

Matt stared back at Neal as he reached behind himself and felt around. He found the handle for the top drawer of his dresser, and pulled it open. Still reaching behind his own back, Matt groped into the back corner, behind his socks, and pulled on a flat, square metal box. He'd gotten a card game in it for his birthday. Bringing the box out, holding it in front of him and feeling around the rim while watching Neal, he popped it open and fingered inside. He felt bills.

Matt held out all the money he had. He did not look at it. Neal reached; Matt pulled the money back.

"You see this. All right? Now you show me my player."

Neal shrugged, reached in his cargo pocket, and pulled out Matt's iPod. He was looking only at the money.

"How much?" Neal said.

Matt, disbelieving this, counted his money. His savings.

"Thirty-three," he said.

"You said *thirty-seven*. You little dick, you said *thirty-seven*."

"Neal," Matt said quietly. "How can you do this? That player was my Christmas present."

"I told you, man, after this one time I have something new. I got it handled, it'll be cool, I can pay you *back*—with *interest*. Pay you *double*. I just have to have this right now. That's all. I *have* to."

"What's thirty-three bucks?"

"It's a *bag*, man, it's a *bag*. I have to have a bag *now*. Will you give me the fucking *money*?"

In Matt's little room where they'd built LEGOs and played PlayStation and fought and talked basketball for hours and hours, Matt said, so softly, "Put it on the bed."

"Give it first. Give me the money."

"No. Put it on the bed."

Neal held the iPod over Matt's bed. His hand was shaking. Staring at the cash in Matt's hands, he let the player fall and lunged for the money. Matt let him take it, then Neal went thundering down the stairs. Matt heard the car door slam and heard the car peel out. He looked out his window and saw the taillights curve fast down the long driveway.

Matt stood there a long time, staring at the darkness. Out there, it was starting to rain.

TWO-MINUTE WARNING

After that night it rained for days. It was a gray rain, chilling and dark. Matt and Katie couldn't do much together. It was too wet and cold to be together outside; and Matt was strange. He wasn't unkind to her. It wasn't the way Sam had warned her guys could get, where they'd be all over you one night and the next day in public it was like they didn't know you. It was more like Katie didn't know him.

He seemed to want to be with her, he would walk with her in the halls and sit with her in the lunchroom, but he barely talked at all. She worried that she had done something, that he wasn't happy with her. But he seemed to need to be with her. He just seemed lost. And as the rain kept falling outside, Katie, who felt it would be disloyal toward Matt to talk to anyone else about this, grew worried and pained and almost as distracted as he was.

They were like two refugees. They wanted to be together, they wanted to stay close and be safe with each other when the rest of the world felt cold and foreign, but what had happened to make them this way, whatever it was, they couldn't, or wouldn't, or just didn't talk about.

The brain trust looked on with almost as much distress. Katie didn't come sit with her friends anymore. She barely talked to them at all. If she and Matt had seemed *happy*, if they'd been talking and laughing and holding hands while gazing deeply and so forth, her three friends would have viewed that with just as much interest and some mixed feelings, but much less alarm. They would have found ways to get involved and share their viewpoints, and they would have been busily protective of Katie, as always—but they wouldn't have felt so uncomfortable and confused. Boyfriend situations had disrupted their circle before, always temporarily. This seemed different. They didn't understand how, exactly, or why.

Then one afternoon, word flew through the school that Matt Shaw had cursed out a teacher. Mrs. Banneman. He had her for math. She was actually fairly nice, not one of the teachers who you'd think would push or goad or antagonize a kid into losing it; but he had. Kids who'd been in the class said Mrs. Banneman had asked in front of everyone if Matt could explain why he hadn't done his homework all week, why he hadn't seemed to be paying the slightest attention that whole class. She hadn't really asked him in a nasty way, the kids said, she just asked—and then Matt went off. He dropped the F-bomb, right there in class. He might even have threatened her, though accounts of this differed, and some seemed dramatized. Anyway he had been pulled out of class and rushed to the office. There was even word that the police were there. Not just the regular school safety officer but someone else, who had come after a while in a plain blue unmarked car that was parked out front. It was clearly a cop car, did you see the antenna? You could tell.

To most kids this was an electrifying scandal. To Tam, Sam, and Hope it was a crisis. Katie was pale and strange. She didn't know what had happened, she told them; she hadn't been there, hadn't seen him, wouldn't talk. She shook her head, hugged herself, and looked away. The other three couldn't help but wonder, with that secret thrill that comes from being on the inside of really bad news, if this thing confirmed their very worst fears about Matt. Then they couldn't help but wonder if Katie, their Katie, had got all tangled up with someone who was headed someplace worse than nowhere, if he wasn't already there.

· · ● · ·

There had been much murmuring and conferencing outside the little room in the main office where Matt was being held. It reminded him of the interrogation room in police TV shows, except that for a while no one seemed able to decide who would interrogate him. His guidance counselor looked in, asked a question or two; then the assistant principal; then the school safety officer.

It was with the safety officer that Matt made his mistake.

The officer, a city patrolman, sat down across the table. He said, "Matt Shaw. Matt Shaw. Where have I heard that name before?"

Matt assumed he knew and was just toying with him. "I didn't take that stuff," he said. "I told the lady I didn't."

"What stuff? What lady?"

"Um . . . you know. The, um . . . the lady."

"You mean Mrs. Banneman? The teacher? Nobody says you took anything, do they?" The cop studied his little notebook. "It's just about what you said."

Oh God, Matt thought.

"Right," he said. "That's right."

"You're talking about something else, aren't you?" the cop said. "Some theft? A lady?" Then something seemed to hit him.

"Oh, wait a minute," he said, and went paging back through his notebook. "I remember now. Here it is: Carolyn Casey. From the detective unit. She was asking about you, wasn't she? Just a week or so ago."

Matt looked down.

"Hang out a little longer, okay?" the cop asked, as if Matt had a choice. "I'm just going to make one call."

The door closed again and Matt sat there miserably.

When the door opened again, maybe twenty minutes later, Carolyn Casey stepped in.

"Well, Matt," she said, "mind if I sit?"

He shrugged. She sat.

"I guess the balloon popped, huh?"

"What?"

"Well," she said. "When a balloon gets pumped too full, so it can't hold any more air, any more pressure, sooner or later it's going to pop, right? You just can't tell where. Could be at home, could be somewhere else. Could be at school."

"Huh."

"Want to tell me what happened?"

He shook his head no.

"I hear you used some strong language."

Matt winced. "God," he said.

Detective Casey cleared her throat. "Matt, I talked to Officer Castilliano about what happened. There's some question about whether you used threatening language as well."

Matt sat up. "I didn't! I just . . . well. I might have said something like 'You better back off.' "

"With some colorful vocab options thrown in, apparently."

Matt smiled, then shook his head again. "I didn't . . ." He looked seriously at the detective. "I didn't mean to. I don't know what happened."

"It's the balloon, Matt. Don't you think? You were trying so hard to hold too much pressure in there. Isn't that possible?"

Matt shrugged, looking down. He didn't want to answer. Then he said, sort of blurting it: "Can I apologize?" Tears jumped into his eyes. He looked down again and fought them back, hard. He sniffled, felt lost.

Carolyn Casey's hand appeared in his fuzzy vision, offering a Kleenex. He took it and cleared his eyes, righted himself. He reminded himself: this person is not your friend. But he wasn't sure, right now, who was. He wanted Katie to be here, then felt really glad she was not. Then he thought, *Oh God, she'll know. They'll all know. But they don't know anything really. I have to tough this out. It's just me against the world.*

"I'm sure you can, Matt—and that would be good," Detective Casey said, and at first Matt wasn't sure what she meant. "Apologizing always helps. But, you know, there are some school policies involved here. If threatening language is used, in times like this, the police have to be called. There's a possibility of a multi-day suspension."

Matt's head shot up. "Multi-*day*?"

"Yeah. It's a tough policy. Obviously your parents would be notified."

"Oh God."

"What would you do with yourself for two or three days? If you were suspended?"

Matt let out a long sigh, shaking his head. "I don't know," he said, almost to himself, "I couldn't stay home . . ."

"Why not?" Detective Casey asked quickly.

Matt realized he'd let something slip. This wasn't his day.

"Well . . . I don't know. I just don't . . . there's nobody there."

"Your brother is there. Isn't he? He's not working, right?"

"Yeah . . ."

"So he could supervise. Couldn't he? I mean if you were suspended."

Matt looked at her. What should he say?

"I guess," he said.

"Unless your brother's kind of preoccupied," Detective Casey said. "With other stuff going on."

Matt looked at the table, at Detective Casey's still-folded hands. Now he had no idea what to say. If he agreed, that would be information, right?

"No he isn't," Matt said.

"Okay then. We would need to speak with him, I mean the school would, to make sure he can properly supervise a suspension."

Matt studied her.

"Wouldn't the school just talk to my parents?" he asked. "Isn't that how they do it?"

Detective Casey straightened in her seat, looking at him. She didn't answer. *Nice try*, Matt thought. *But give me a little credit. I'm not stupid.* He wondered if he'd won that round.

"Matt, do you know about the two-minute warning?"

"The what?"

"We call it the two-minute warning," she said. She leaned over the table, like she was going to give him inside information. "When you see traffic going in and out of a neighbor's house, or even maybe your house, that keeps coming and going, but people only stay for like two minutes—or less—we call that the two-minute warning. It means there may be something going on there that maybe shouldn't be going on."

Matt shrugged again.

"Matt? Is there any chance that kind of traffic could be happening at your house?"

"I don't know. I don't go home. After school, I mean."

"Oh, I know. Any chance this could be why you don't go home?"

Matt didn't answer.

"Matt, we do hear things," she said. "Lately what we hear, just in the past few days in fact, is that all of a sudden there's been a lot of this kind of traffic in and out of your home. One of your neighbors called about it. Said they thought it was strange."

Matt wondered, *Who? KJ? He wouldn't. Would he?*

"I can tell you we're starting to see a pattern here," Detective Casey said. "It's a pretty familiar pattern, actually. Can I tell you about that?"

Again Matt didn't answer. Inside himself he was backing as far away as he could. He didn't want to hear, didn't want to respond. Didn't want to be here.

"It's like this," she said. "There may be some signs, at first, of changing behavior by someone in a family. Maybe they isolate themselves. Maybe they stop doing things they always loved to do; maybe they kind of cut themselves off. Don't talk. You know?"

Did she mean him? Did they still think it was him?

"Now, that alone isn't a huge red flag—especially with teenagers," she said. "You guys go through changes, right? But then, the next step in the pattern *is* a red flag. That's when things start disappearing from a home. Things that can be easily taken, and easily sold. And maybe to us it doesn't much look like these are burglaries from outside."

Matt was staring at her now. She held his eyes.

"So someone in the family—it's possible that someone really needs money. And maybe after a while this thing of stealing from the family doesn't work anymore. Maybe the police get called, or there's some other kind of bad scene. And maybe the needs of the person for money grow bigger. So next, before long, maybe right away even, there's this new traffic. In and out of the house. Almost like somebody's . . . selling something."

Oh God, thought Matt. *Oh God. "I got something new,"* Neal had said. *"It's just getting started."*

Oh no.

"Matt, you're in some trouble here, right now in school," Detective Casey said, "but it's not really that huge a trouble, is it? You popped off in class. In a way it suggests to me that you're feeling a lot of pressure or stress. Or worry. If you were doing something to fuzz out or medicate that stress, you probably wouldn't have that buildup to where you'd pop off. You know? The balloon wouldn't be so tight. I don't think it's you, Matt."

"Huh?"

"I don't think it's you. I don't think you stole from your parents, and I don't think, at this point, that you are involved with this traffic at your house in the daytime. In fact, I think what's been going on at your house probably is the reason why you've been staying away. I don't think it's you—but I think you and I both have a pretty good idea who it is."

A kind of relief flooded Matt. He was surprised by the feeling. But he held himself tight and didn't say anything.

"Matt, if I'm interpreting the situation right, it's completely understandable why you'd be under a lot of stress, and why you'd be really worried," Detective Casey said. "It's understandable why you'd pop off in school. That doesn't make it okay, but it's understandable. In fact, I'm pretty sure I could make the school understand, too, if you'll just work with me here."

Uh-oh, Matt thought.

"Matt, if what we think may be going on at your house is what is going on, the person at the center of it is in a very, very serious situation. This is not only extremely illegal, if it is what we suspect—it can also be deadly. In several different ways. The material in question is totally deadly. We can say the same for some of the people involved with it. We're talking about a very serious danger here, Matt. Do you want someone you love to be in that kind of danger?"

He looked at her a long time. She waited.

"No," he said.

"Okay," she said. "So what can you tell me?"

He just felt miserable.

"I don't know," he said finally. "I don't know anything. I stay away." He looked back at her almost pleadingly.

"The people coming in and out of your home," she said. "Do you recognize any of them?"

"No. I don't even see them. I told you . . ."

"I know. You stay away. I don't blame you," Detective Casey said. "Have you taken any messages? Heard any messages on an answering machine?"

"He has a cell phone."

"Oh, sure. What's that number?"

"I . . . I don't know."

"You don't know his cell phone number?" She looked skeptical.

"I *don't*," he said. "I don't call him. He doesn't want me to call him."

" 'He,' of course," Detective Casey said, "being your brother."

Matt felt his face heat up.

"Neal Shaw," Detective Casey said. "Rutland High School, graduated last year. Big hoop star, of course. The last person anyone might expect to be . . ."

She let that sentence trail off. She sat back, like she was waiting for him to fill the silence.

"I don't know the people," Matt said, almost desperately. "I don't see what they're . . . I just don't see."

"But you know." She sat up straight and leaned in close. "You know what's going on in there. You know why people are coming and going. You know full well. Don't you?"

"I don't! I've never *seen* anything! I just know . . . he told me . . ."

"What?"

Oh God. Oh God. Me against the world. Stay tight.

"Nothing," he said.

"Did he ever steal from you?" she asked.

"What?"

"Bingo," she said. "He did, didn't he? I can see by the look on your face."

"No," he said. "No. Nothing happened."

"Hmm," she said, studying him. "You know, Matt, right at

this moment I think you're not quite telling me the truth. And you know what? You're not really that great at lying." She stared steadily at him, boring into him quietly, letting that last word sink in.

"Do you understand it's not okay to lie to a police detective?" she asked. When he didn't answer, she said, "You know something else? Nothing's off limits to a heroin addict. Nothing. They'll do anything, say anything, steal anything, use anyone, to get a hit. Know why? 'Cause the drug, the heroin, Matt, it takes them over. It totally takes over. It's like that person you knew, that person you loved, is just not there anymore."

"Yeah!" Matt said, before he could think. "I know."

"Sure." Carolyn Casey nodded. "And that's it, isn't it? There's heroin in your house. That's the drug that's got your brother, and that's why he stole from everyone. Including you."

"No," he said.

She raised her eyebrows. "Matt . . ."

"He did not steal from me."

"No?"

"No. He didn't."

"He tried though, huh," she said. "Maybe you caught him. Or something. Right?"

Matt shrugged. He was mad now. He felt tricked. He wasn't giving her one more crumb. He stared at the table.

"Must have felt awful," she said. "I know you know what I mean, about not knowing who the hell this person is anymore."

The curse word startled Matt, and he looked up. Detective Casey's expression had softened.

"It's all right, Matt," she said. "You haven't given me anything we weren't already pretty sure about. But now, do you remember what I said, about how dangerous this situation is for him? Did you hear that?"

Matt nodded. He had.

"Have you still got my card? Remember, I gave it to you?"

"Uh, yeah. But no. I don't think so."

"All right then," she said, and fished out another one. "Here you go. Now, it's incredibly important that you hold on to this card, that you keep it with you. All right? I want you to keep this on your person. Got a wallet?"

"Yeah."

"Okay. Put it in there. Can I see you do that?"

Matt pulled out his flat, empty excuse for a wallet. He slipped the card in where there might be money, if he still had any.

"Great," she said. "Keep it there. Keep the wallet with you. All right? If anything occurs where your brother is in danger, or you're in danger, or anyone else is—or if you see something happening that you want help with, that I can help with in any way—you call me. Just call me. Anytime. Don't even think; just call. Okay?"

Matt didn't answer. He shrugged. But he put the wallet in his pocket.

She sighed. "Okay, Matt. We're just about done here. You promise you'll keep that card?"

Matt didn't answer.

"You know, I still think you're a decent kid," she said. "I

still don't think you're part of this. In fact, I think you want this situation to come out okay. I think you really want that. Don't you?"

"Yes," Matt said. It was true.

"So we both want the same thing. I mean, if you think about it, I want your brother to be safe, and I want that stuff out of your house. Just like you."

Matt nodded. Hearing that loosened him a little bit. "When you said about the two-minute warning, before," he said to her, "I thought you meant football."

"Well, yeah—and here's how that connects. In football, the two-minute warning means the game is going into its last phase. Right? It means if you're going to make a difference, make an impact, make it come out the right way, then the time is coming pretty soon when you have to do something."

She studied him.

"Try trusting somebody, Matt," she said. "Maybe the person you've trusted and looked to for a long time isn't the one you can count on right now—but that doesn't mean you can't trust somebody." She paused. "Try telling someone the truth."

He wouldn't look at her.

"Even if you pretend something is not happening," she said, more gently now, "it is still happening."

He nodded. "I know," he said.

"Think about it," she said. "And keep the card. All right?"

Matt nodded.

"Okay." She waved toward the door. "We're set here, Matt. I'll work it out with the school. You can go."

ONE ON ONE

As school ended that day, Hope found Katie alone in the cafeteria. She was sitting at an empty table.

"Coots," Hope whispered, sitting down beside her. Katie just nodded.

For a while they sat quietly, side by side. No one else was in the big room. Through the cafeteria doors, Hope could see the hectic, noisy flow of kids out in the front hall, leaving school. In here, finally, she said: "Do you know what's going on?"

Katie shook her head. "He's still in the principal's office. I thought maybe I could wait till he gets let out, but . . . I don't know. I don't know if he'll want to see me or anything."

"Why wouldn't he want to see you?"

Katie hung her head. "I don't know."

Hope studied her friend carefully. "Do you know what's really going on?" she asked. "With him?"

"No. Why, do you?"

"No, but there's something. There has to be something. Don't you think?"

"I don't know." Katie sighed and took a breath. "I'm not supposed to ask," she said.

"He told you that? He said you couldn't ask him?"

"Well . . . not exactly. But he sort of did. It was pretty clear." She looked up helplessly.

"You think there's something he doesn't want to tell?" Hope asked.

Katie had to let it out. Her balloon was too full, too.

"Yes, but I don't know what. I don't," she said again, as if maybe Hope wouldn't believe her.

But Hope said, "Katie." Katie was staring past Hope now, at nothing. "Listen to me," Hope said. "Are you listening?"

Katie nodded.

"You need to ask him," Hope said.

Katie didn't answer.

"I mean, Katie," Hope said, "you've never not asked questions. Right? I mean, that's who you are."

Katie shrugged.

"Well, it's true," Hope said. "And now you're supposed to just not do that? About something that might be really big? I mean, what's up with that?"

Katie wasn't looking at her. "I don't know," she said. She was holding herself in now, trying to keep something she didn't understand from spilling over.

"It's like you're supposed to give up who you are, just so you can be with him," Hope said. "But, I mean, Katie, how can that ever work? How can you be happy with someone if a whole big part of you isn't allowed to be there?"

Tears began slipping down Katie's face. "There's so much *pressure*," she whispered. "It's so hard."

"What's hard?"

"Being in love."

"Are you in love?"

Katie nodded. Her face was pure misery, the tears pouring down now.

"He's all I can think about, all the time," she said. "When I'm not with him I can't stand it, I don't know what to do. All I can think about is when we'll talk, when we'll see each other, how he feels, what he'll say. But when we do see each other, it's like we can't talk at all anymore. At first we could, but something happened and I don't know what it was. I don't know if it was me and I can't ask and he won't talk to me. I know I have to ask him what's the matter, but it's got so that . . . it's like I just *can't*. And I don't get why. At first I thought I understood him, I mean in a real way—but now I feel like I don't understand anything. I can't *stand* it."

Katie was sobbing helplessly now. Hope waited till she'd settled a little. Then she said, "Be you, Katie. Okay? You need to be you. Ask him what's going on. *Ask* him."

Katie sat with this. She knew Hope would have thought about it before saying anything. She knew that of all her friends, it was Hope who made the deepest sense.

"Okay," she said, and felt better for having said it. "Okay."

Hope stood up. "Come over to my house for a while," she

said. "We'll do something mindless and fattening. It'll be *so* good for you. You can call him later."

"Do you think? Shouldn't I wait here?"

"No. Come on. He'll probably be embarrassed anyway. You can call him later."

"Okay. I will," Katie said as she got up, too.

· · ● · ·

As he was leaving school that afternoon, a worried KJ was surprised to find himself approached by a girl.

It wasn't just any girl—it was Tamra Kaplan, a major figure at Jeffords Junior High. She was taller than him, she'd been a starter on the girls' ninth-grade basketball team, and she was someone that most people either admired and thought was cool, or put down behind her back. Because they were jealous, probably. KJ and Tam had been friendly, on a polite level, and he was one of those who basically admired her, but that was all. She had never sought him out before.

"Hey," she said now, coming up as he stood on the patio out front.

"Hey."

"You and me," Tam said. "We need to talk."

"Well . . . okay."

Tam looked him up and down. Then she smiled. It was a friendly smile, but challenging.

"You know what, it's open gym this afternoon and there's hardly anybody in there," she said, nodding back at the tall, blocklike part of the school building that held the basketball courts. "You used to play, right?"

"Hey. I play all the time."

"Bet you can't beat me," she said, still smiling.

KJ pulled himself up to his full five feet, five inches.

"Bet I can try," he said, and grinned right back up at her.

Tam was right—the gym was almost empty, except for a clutch of nonathletic kids at the front end who were playing ball in a messy way, fooling around using up time after school. Tam strode to the far end of the court and stood alone beneath the glass backboard there. The bleachers were pushed back, so the gym was wide and empty on both sides of her.

She turned to face him, hands on her hips.

"This is *my* house," she said, grinning at him.

"Jeez." KJ smiled back as he walked toward her on the court. "Where do you get that stuff?"

Tamra laughed, once. Then she trotted to the open door of the equipment room. She went in, then stuck her head back out.

"Girls' ball or guys'?"

KJ shrugged. "You choose."

She nodded. "Guys'," she said, and came out dribbling a full-sized basketball.

They were both wearing T-shirts, shorts, and sneakers because it was a warm day outside, and because basketball clothes were what, if they could, they wore. They shot around for a few minutes, Tamra swooping at the basket in her excitement, KJ chunkily practicing his solid new jump shot. Neither had forgotten what they were worried about, which was Matt for KJ and, of course, Katie for Tam; but they weren't thinking about that now. KJ was thinking, *Go up straight*, and *Solid moves. Play a solid game.* Girl or no girl, this was a chance to prove himself against a ninth-grade starter. As he worked his shot he kept himself focused on what Matt had shown him, which he had been practicing ever since. *Make a strong move*, he told himself, *then square up, and go up straight.*

They shot free throws for first possession. Tam missed hers, KJ hit his. She flipped him the ball and bent into the defender's stance.

"Winner's outs?" KJ asked.

"Sure," Tam said. She straightened up, smiling. "Should I take it now, or wait?"

"Ha ha," said KJ. He started dribbling, and she was ready. He charged right and she was on him, all arms and legs. KJ reversed and she was there, too. He backed off, still dribbling, and looked at her. Tam's eyes were glittering.

"Got a Plan B?" she said.

KJ switched to his left hand and bulled past her shoulder, smacking it with his as he went. He had a lane to the basket and went for it as Tam bore down from behind. He lifted up a left-handed layup just beyond her fast-closing arms and it went in.

KJ was back above the key. "Winner's outs," he said. "Check?"

Tam nodded, not smiling now. He bounced it to her and she bounced it back, then bent and was ready.

They went at it. Tam's defense was overaggressive, which probably threw most people off, KJ figured—but he found that if he charged hard at an angle, she would scramble, pursuing; then he could pull up, square up, and rise in one motion, spinning the shot off his fingers while she was still flailing to catch up. The first time he tried this, with the score 1–1, he was amazed that it worked. It went in. *Thanks, dude,* he said to Matt in his mind.

But then mostly it was combat. Tam was everywhere, her long arms reaching and annoying. When she'd force him to miss she would sweep in the rebound and be ready to go, dribbling to the top of the key and bouncing on her feet while KJ rushed to get there and gasped for breath. She was in better shape than he was, she'd been running all winter and she had the long legs. Her game was to dribble at you, then turn to spin off you, whirling toward the basket. If you didn't move your feet fast enough, she'd get around you and score—or else she'd back you up with the spinning move and then she would try it again, spinning off you, working in closer, finally launching her shot.

Tam liked the bank shot and she was a little wild with it, a little messy and undisciplined. She could have used Matt's wisdom, too. But she brought so much *energy* to the game. She'd come at you and come at you. After she put up each of her wild shots, KJ laid solid body checks on her to keep her away from the backboard; but he couldn't keep her long arms from reaching over him to snatch away the rebound, and then she would be coming at him all over again.

It was 8–5 Tam, game to 11. KJ had the ball. Time to try the crossover.

He dribbled right, not too high this time, and feinted that way. She went for it, her arms out wide; he slipped the dribble between them and charged after it. But Tam caught up and went reaching across KJ's body for a steal as he drove for the layup; KJ pulled the ball away from her fingers and went up hard with Tam still bending over him on the fly. His elbow smashed into her nose, and suddenly there was blood.

"Oh *no*," he said. Tam, who had staggered backward, seemed stunned. She stood there blinking as the blood started to pour. "Your nose!" KJ said. He pulled his T-shirt over his head and held it, wadded up, against her face. He reached up with his other hand to cradle the back of her head. He said, "Come on, okay? You need to lie down."

Tam nodded and took the T-shirt to hold it on her own. KJ guided her, his hand on her shoulder now, until they had reached the one bench that was pulled out from the retracted bleachers.

"Lie down here," KJ said gently. "Right here. Okay?"

Tam nodded. She sat down sideways on the bench and lay slowly backward, holding the shirt against her face, until she was horizontal. She gazed woozily up at the lights.

"Crap," she said fuzzily through the shirt. "I had you."

"Oh, I think not—that was my signature move," KJ said. "I'll get some paper towels or something, all right?"

But she waved no. She lay there awhile, holding the cloth

185

on her face. KJ sat quietly beside her. Finally, carefully, she tried sitting up.

Tam pulled the shirt away, looked at it. A big patch of it was soaked with red.

"Your shirt's wrecked," she said.

"That's okay."

"Do you have to go home half-naked? 'Cause, you know, people shouldn't have to see that."

"I have a jacket," KJ said, smiling.

"Good. How's my nose?"

KJ peered. "I think it's stopped."

"Look broken?"

He shrugged. "I never saw a broken nose, but yours looks pretty normal. Well, not exactly *normal*. It looks like your nose."

Tam pulled back the wadded shirt like she might fling it at him. "Ow," she said, and cupped her nose. She felt it with her fingertips.

"I think it's okay," she said. "So. Ready to go? Your ball or mine?"

"No *way*," said KJ. "You take it easy right now. We can finish this sometime, if you want to. If you think you can withstand my furious comeback."

She grinned. "Okay. Tomorrow. That gives you a whole day to go on thinking you have a chance."

"Tomorrow would be fine," he said.

"No open gym tomorrow, though."

"We can play in my driveway," KJ said. "I have a pretty decent court."

"Okay." Tam nodded. "You gonna wear a shirt for once?"

KJ grinned. "I guess so."

"But not one of those stupid Michael Jordan shirts, all right?"

"*Hey.*"

"I mean, no offense," she said. "But let it go."

"You're just scared it'll give me an edge."

"Oh yeah, that's it, all right. So . . . after school tomorrow? Is your house far?"

"Well, it's not that close but it's walkable. I'll show you."

"Deal," she said. "I feel a little dizzy."

"Lie back down. It's okay."

She did. Staring up again, she said, "That was fun."

"Yeah."

"You play okay, for a boy. How come you didn't go out this year?"

"I did."

"Oh."

"I'm getting better, though," KJ said. "Next year." He almost mentioned Michael Jordan's tenth-grade experience but decided not to.

"We could work on it," Tam said. "Your game, I mean. And mine."

He glanced at her, surprised. "You mean that?"

"Sure, why not? That way I get multiple chances to kick your butt."

KJ nodded. "Cool." He stared across the now-empty gym.

"What'd you want to talk about before?" he asked. "I bet I can guess."

"Bet you can."

They didn't say anything for a while. He sat, looking across the gym, and she lay looking up.

"She's my best friend," Tam finally said.

KJ nodded. "I know. He's pretty much mine. However wacked out he is these days."

"So what's up with that? How come he didn't go out, a player like that? Do you know?"

KJ nodded, but squeezed his mouth tight.

Tam sat up. "We're kind of scared," she said. "Her friends, I mean. We don't know what's going on. Is he into anything, you know, like dangerous? Or illegal? Or anything?"

KJ shook his head. He hadn't said anything to anybody, outside the discussions in his own family. But things were getting bad over there, and he knew it.

"He isn't," KJ said. "His brother is."

"His brother? The one who was all-state?"

"Yeah."

"I don't get it," Tam said. She felt her nose. "Ow."

"Well, basically, his brother's a junkie now."

"A *what*?"

"A junkie. You know. He does heroin."

Tam let go her nose. "Oh my God," she said.

"Yeah. Matt thinks nobody knows. But I live next door, and I have an older sister. She's messed around with some stuff, though never the really serious stuff—but she knows some of the people who hang around Neal's house in the daytime. When their parents aren't home, right? Basically they're dirt-balls. My sister says they're all junkies."

"Oh God," Tam said.

"It happens a lot around here," KJ said. "That's what Shelly says. My sister."

Tam nodded and winced. "What about Matt?"

"I'm pretty positive he doesn't mess with that stuff. He stays away from his house after school 'cause he doesn't want to deal with it, you know? With those people. With that situation. I wouldn't want to either."

"So that's why he walks?"

"Yeah."

"But why didn't he play?"

KJ shrugged. "If you'd seen how close him and Neal were. I mean, they were *real* brothers—especially with basketball. That was like their bond, you know? I think when Neal didn't get a scholarship, to play in college, he sort of fell in a hole. Then before you knew it he was into this stuff. It made Matt just not want to play anymore. That's what I think anyway. Maybe Matt was hoping it would get Neal's attention or some-thing, or maybe he just couldn't deal with it. He didn't want to play anymore 'cause it was what they did. The two of them. You know?"

Tam thought. "Yeah," she said. "I get it. But, so, what about what happened today?"

KJ shook his head. "I probably shouldn't say this, but . . . the last couple weeks there's been a whole new kind of flow, in and out of their house in the daytime. My sister said the word is Neal's dealing now. My folks actually called the police about it. This lady detective came to talk to us. I'm not supposed to say anything about it, 'cause it's an investigation."

"Can't they just go in there and arrest somebody? If they know?"

"Well, I think they don't know. They suspect."

"So? Shouldn't that be enough?"

"No. See, they can't go in there without a warrant, right? That's what the lady detective said. You have to get a warrant from a judge, and the judge wants something solid. Suspicious traffic and rumors in the druggie world aren't totally enough."

"Huh."

"The detective said she was hoping for a breakthrough pretty soon," KJ said. "I don't know what she meant, exactly. But something."

"And then what happens to Matt?"

"I don't know—but I think he's been really scared about his brother. He doesn't want to be the one to rat him out, you know? I think he thinks he's protecting him. But at this point the whole thing's gone pretty far. I really don't know what's going to happen."

Tam shook her head. "Wow. Do you think Katie knows? She must know."

"I bet she doesn't," KJ said. "Matt's been totally secretive about everything. If he knew I knew anything, he'd probably freak."

"But wouldn't he tell his girlfriend?"

"He's a guy," KJ said. "We don't really *talk* like you do. And anyway, if you had this stuff going on in your family, when everybody thinks your family is so great, would you want your *girlfriend* to know about it?"

"Yes," Tam said. "I tell my friends everything."

"That's because you're girls," KJ said.

"Yes. Thank God. I mean, how can he not *talk* to some-body about this? If he knows, how can he not tell somebody?"

· · ● · ·

"Matt . . . please," Katie said on the phone that evening. It was a couple of hours later, about the same time that Tamra, who had come home from the gym and had dinner, was getting on the phone as well, first to call Hope and then to call Sam.

"What?" said Matt.

"Please talk to me," Katie said. "Please. Matt. I need you to talk to me."

"About what?" Matt said, though he knew.

Katie let out a long sigh. "Matt," she said, and she started to cry. *Oh God, don't,* she thought.

"You have to tell me what's going on," she said. "You have to tell me what's the matter. I know there's something, and I know we sort of agreed I wouldn't ask and we wouldn't talk about it. But, Matt, you're in *trouble.*"

"I'm not. They let me go. I didn't get suspended or any-thing."

"But you're still in trouble, Matt. You think I can't tell?

Something's not right. I know you don't want to talk about it, but I think it's gotten bad. And now it's like we can't ever talk about anything."

She waited. No answer.

"Matt. You can trust me. I *care* about you. Whatever it is . . ." She took a deep breath. "Whatever it is, I don't care. I mean I'll still care. I will. I do."

Another silence.

"You can trust me," Katie repeated.

There was a long silence. Finally Matt said, "You can't tell anybody."

"I won't."

"I mean *anybody*. Your girlfriends or anybody."

"I won't, Matt. I promise. You can *trust* me."

Silence again. Katie made herself just breathe.

"Okay," he finally said. "It's . . . well . . . I don't know."

"This is really hard," Katie said. "I know."

"It's my brother," he said. And then he told her everything.

He told her everything at pretty much the same time that Tam, who had promised nobody anything and was just worried about her friend, told Hope and then told Sam what she had learned from KJ. When that conversation was over, Sam, who could hardly believe what she'd just heard, started making phone calls and instant-messaging people at the same time.

FAST BREAK

Darryl Casey came up to Matt at his locker during the first change of classes next morning, between periods one and two. Darryl and Matt were not friends, never had been. So Matt instantly felt wary when he looked up to see Darryl walking toward him with an eager gleam in his eyes.

"Dude," said Darryl, shaking his head in pretend sympathy as he pushed one hand through his thick curve of dark blond hair. "Whoa. This is tough."

"What is?"

"I'm really sorry, man," said Darryl. But he didn't look sorry; he looked even more self-satisfied than usual. "But hey. At least everybody gets it now."

"Gets what?" Matt felt tiny heat pops flash down his chest and arms.

"Why you've been so weird, dude! I mean, hey, I'd be acting a little different, too, if my brother was dealing H."

It hit Matt like a board in the face. He took Darryl by the shoulders and slammed him against the next locker. Darryl's eyes went wide, then he winced as Matt held him there.

"Ow! Dude . . . *ow*. The lock's in my *back*, man . . ."

"Where'd you hear that?"

"Ow. What?"

"Where'd you *hear* that?" People were stopping and turning in the hall to look. Matt didn't care. Darryl squirmed; Matt shoved him up tighter against the metal. He got in close and spoke low.

"Casey, if you want to live, tell me where you heard that."

"I don't know, man. It's all over school! Some girl told people last night. Okay? Will you let me *go*?" He squirmed again.

Matt felt all the strength drain out of him, just drain right down through his feet. His hands went lax, and Darryl, his face red, twisted away and hurried off down the hall. Matt didn't watch. He stood looking at the blank gray metal of the locker door, which slowly went blurry in his vision. Everything was flushed away. Everything. Then he began to fill again, with a focused anger.

He didn't think; he walked. He knew, he felt, that everybody was looking at him. That everybody knew. In his red-burning anger there was only one thing to do.

He knew Katie's next class and found her outside it. When she saw him coming fast, she lit up; then, when she saw his expression, her face changed.

"What's wrong?" she asked.

Matt leaned in close. Then he looked around. People were too near. He pointed with his head down the hall.

"Matt, I have class." But as he walked away from the classroom door, she followed. She held her books tight against her chest.

When he stopped, Katie whispered, "What is it?"

Matt glanced past her. People were distant enough now, though several were sneaking looks their way. He looked in her face, and his eyes were burning. He spoke low and close.

"You bitch."

Katie went white. "What?"

"You *bitch*. I *trusted* you."

"Matt . . . what? You *can* trust me, I . . ."

"Don't lie. Do not *lie*. You told everyone. Soon as you got off with me you got back on that phone and you told *everyone*."

Horrified, Katie opened her mouth but nothing came out.

"We're done," said Matt. "We are *done*, all right? I can't believe you did that to me—I can't believe I trusted you. You just wrecked my life and you probably wrecked my brother's life, too. What did he ever do to you? Why did I ever trust you? I can't believe I was that *stupid*."

Katie's wide eyes went soft behind a welling wetness. "Matt . . . I would never . . ."

"Don't even *try*," he hissed at her. "Just get out of my life. I don't want to see you, I don't want to talk to you. I don't want to hear you lie again. *Ever*."

"Oh, Matt . . ."

"Oh, and here," he said. He dug in his pocket and pulled something out. He opened his hand and flung it down; as the thing hit the floor it broke into bits of black stone, once protective, now shattered and skittering apart.

"There's your stupid rock," he said as he spun and stalked away.

HUMAN NATURE

didn't mean for you to tell everybody! I just meant to tell us! Why'd you tell *everybody*?"

Tamra was leaning over the cafeteria table toward Samantha. Sam was red-faced and hunched over, folding into herself.

"I didn't! I just told . . . a few people."

"You know what this school is like!" Tam said. "Now it's everywhere!"

"I didn't *mean* to," Sam said, and began to sob.

The cafeteria was busy and crowded. Hope came up, holding a tray that had only orange juice on it. Nobody could eat.

"Where is she?" Hope asked Tam, ignoring Sam, who was crying helplessly now.

"Home," said Tam. "She had hysterics right in the hall, right after he dumped her. They had to send her to the nurse, and her mom had to leave work and come get her."

"She was hysterical?"

"Totally. Oh, Sam, will you stop?"

"I can't!"

"Did you see her?" Hope asked.

"Yeah, for a minute. I went to the nurse's office after social studies. She could barely talk. I finally got out of her what happened, sort of. He heard from somebody that everybody suddenly knows about his brother. He assumed she told, 'cause last night she finally got him to trust her and tell her what's going on."

"Oh *God*," Sam said. She flopped her head down on her arms, and her luxurious golden hair fanned over the table.

"It's really my fault," Tam told Hope. "Sam knew because I told her." She shook her head bitterly. "How could I not realize what would happen?"

"It's nobody's fault—it's human nature," Hope said. "Something like this is going to get out. But now what do we do?"

Tam sat back and thought. "You know," she said after a moment, "she's really better off. I mean she's traumatized right now, but if this is the stuff that's going on in his life, she would have to break up with him anyway. Right?"

"But it's not him. It's his brother," Hope said.

"But he's obviously wrapped up in it. I mean, he's been keeping the secret, right? Doesn't that make him, you know, an accomplice?"

"I thought it made him enigmatic," Hope said, glancing at Sam's wash of blond hair splayed across the table.

Sam's head popped up. "Is *that* my fault, too? Is *everything* my fault?"

"Oh, Sam," said Hope.

"You do have an eye for the idiots," Tam tossed in, and Sam's head flopped back down.

"Oh, good one, Tamra," said Hope. Tam shrugged.

"He thought he had to protect his brother," Hope said. "How would you like to be in a situation like that?"

"I would not, and she shouldn't be either," Tam said. "That's what I'm saying. She's out of it now, and we have to get her to stay out of it. I mean, be devastated, fall apart, whatever. Just don't go back to him."

Sam's head came up. "He dumped her," she said. "Just like that, right? He didn't ask for her side or anything. Right?"

"That's right."

Sam shook her head.

"I wouldn't go back for just that reason," she said.

"You wouldn't?" asked Hope.

"No. I wouldn't." Her face was set.

"Why, Samantha," said Hope. "That's different."

"It is not," she said. "You have to have self-respect."

Tam stood up. "I'm calling her."

"Now?"

"Yeah. I'm not hungry anyway." She groped in her pocket. "We have ten minutes before class. I have to *do* something. Hey, who has a quarter? I only have one."

"See? We need cell phones," Sam said as she handed over a coin. "This is just why."

· · ● · ·

Katie answered on the second ring.

"Hi," said Tam.

"Oh," said Katie, sounding deflated. Tam knew she had hoped it was him. Tam asked, "Are you all right?"

Katie didn't answer. Tam could hear her breath catching in small spasms.

"Katie. Sweetie. Is it really bad?"

Tam heard a sniffle.

"Yes," said Katie in a faraway voice.

"What can I do?"

"Would you talk to him?"

"Would I . . ."

"If you would just *talk* to him," Katie said, urgently now. "Tell him it wasn't me. Could you? If he could just know it wasn't me."

Tam knew she could tell Matt more than that. But this was not what she had wanted to talk to Katie about.

"Katie . . . don't you think . . ."

"Would you? Please? Tam?" Katie sounded like she was fading backward. Like she was lost inside a cave.

"Uh . . . I could try. I guess."

"Oh God . . . *thank* you, Tam."

"Well . . ."

"Will you tell me what he says? Will you call me, or . . . or come here right after school? Darcy says I can't leave till she gets home from work. I can't go out."

"Is she furious?"

"Oh, pretty much. She said, 'This is the last time I get pulled out of work because of a *boy*.' "

"Wasn't it the first time?" Tam asked.

"That too."

The bell rang.

"Tam," said Katie, "I heard the bell, but . . . call me. Okay? After you talk to him. As *soon* as you talk to him. Okay?"

"All right. I'll try."

Tam hung up and walked heavily to class.

· · ● · ·

Tam had Matt in mid-afternoon French. He was there, looking more closed-up and solitary than usual. When the period ended, as other kids evacuated the room she strode up to Matt.

"We need to talk," she said.

He shoved his book in his backpack, said nothing, and dodged past her. She fought down irritation, then went after him.

In the hall Tam stepped past Matt, spun around, and held up her hands.

"Whoa," she said. "Just *whoa*, all right? We need to talk."

"No we don't. I don't even know you," he said, trying to dodge around again. But Tam sidestepped to block him.

"I'm her best friend," she said, "and you got it wrong. I can totally understand why it would seem the way it seems, but it's not that way. It's not, all right? If you'll just . . ."

"Look," Matt said, "I couldn't care less who's friends with who. My life is wrecked now, okay? My whole family's life is going to be wrecked. Can *you* put that back together?"

"But . . ."

"Can you tell everybody in this school that they don't know what they think they know? Can you put it all back the way it was?"

"Well . . . but it's not her fault," Tam said.

"Oh yeah? Well it's not *mine*," he said. "So whose fault is it? Yours?"

This was the moment when Tam might have explained. But with this boy's attitude right in her face, what she wanted to do was smack him. Hard. He deserved it, too. Or else she'd have liked to march him to the gym and challenge him. Right then and there. *You and me, quitter boy. Let's go.* The last thing she wanted to do, at this particular moment, was tell him yes, it was her, she had made a mistake.

She said nothing.

"That's what I figured," Matt said as he stepped past her and walked away fast.

Tam stood there, watching, and fighting back the urge to run up and smack him in the back of the head.

EXITS

This time, before her last class of the day, Tam borrowed her language-arts teacher's phone. She cupped her free hand over her mouth and kept her voice low, so no one would hear as kids streamed and then straggled into class.

Katie asked, "Did you talk to him? Oh Tam, you talked to him. Right?"

"Yeah."

"What'd he *say*? Does he understand it wasn't me? What'd he say?"

"He . . . wouldn't let me explain. He's being a jerk, Katie. I really think you're . . ."

"You didn't tell him?"

"He wouldn't *let* me. Listen, Katie, I can't talk long. But I really think . . ."

"Oh *God*." Tam heard a spasm. Sobbing.

"Katie . . ."

"I have to find him. I have to *talk* to him."

Cupping her hand tighter, Tam whispered urgently, "*Don't. No.* Katie . . ."

She heard a click. She stared at the phone, then set it down.

As soon as school ended, Tam, Sam, and Hope went straight to the front patio. They stood there beside the steps, on the stone ledge where Katie had watched Matt meet Detective Casey for the first time. They watched everybody leave school, and they also kept looking down Library Avenue, toward the Grove Street light.

"She's got to come this way. Maybe you should go over by the buses," Tam said to Hope. "Make sure he doesn't come out the side door."

"What if I see him?"

"Then come get me. Fast. We have to talk to him before she does—or talk to her before she finds him. We *have* to." If Tam saw Katie, she was going to stop her—tell her she *had* to let this go. Let him go. If she saw Matt, she would tell him . . . well . . . she wasn't sure what she would tell him. The thought of talking to him at all annoyed her; but she had to do something.

Sam was still peering toward the traffic light. "I don't see her."

"Keep looking. Walk toward the light and watch from there. Okay?"

"Okay."

Sam walked down School Street, the afternoon light dancing off her hair. Hope was already going the other way, dodging kids as she threaded her way up the sidewalk toward the idling yellow schoolbuses.

But Matt went out a back door. He didn't want to see anyone, not anyone in the whole school. So he slipped out a door that kids used to go to the fenced-in field and playground behind the school when they had free time. Matt walked along the back streets that ran in the same direction as Grove Street, going away from the city center, until he knew he was well ahead of anyone. Then he walked straight out on Grove. He kept on on going, way out past his house, past the country club, past everything.

He only wanted to walk and walk, to leave everyone as far behind as he possibly could. He clamped on his headphones and turned his player up loud. He chose a song he didn't always like, a Jai Quest song:

> *Yo! Bitch tellin' you she's for real*
> *Say I don't think so, you can't steal*
> *What I got—'cause it's all mine*
> *I did the crime but I ain't doin' the time*
> *I give you what I want to when I want it*
> *'Cause a woman try to take it*
> *If she tell you that she loves you*
> *Watch out because she's fakin'*
> *I got places got to go to*
> *Ain't nobody sayin' no, too*
> *Tell her baby I ain't stayin'*
> *I just stopped in for some playin'*

I will take it if I wanna,
I know you wanna give it,
But then I'm goin', I got shows
Say she's waitin', I say no—hah!
Say you love me, I just laugh
Don't need no one, got my stash

Baby I ain't stayin'
I just stopped by
For some playin'
Hey baby
Ain't that right?
Gonna be waitin' for me tonight?

As Tam sat by the patio steps keeping watch, a stocky boy came out the front door.

"Hey," said KJ.

"Oh. Hey."

Then KJ sat down next to her. He leaned his forearms on his knees, so his head was down below hers.

"Sooo," he said. "Everybody's talking about Matt Shaw today."

"Um . . ."

"And his brother."

Tam said nothing, but she tensed. She hadn't been thinking about how KJ would react.

"He's my friend," KJ said, down low so only she could hear. "I told you that, right?"

"Yes. You told me that."

"So what happened?"

Tam took a breath. She looked around; nobody else was listening. Kids were just going by.

"It was my fault," she said as she kept an eye on the crowd. "There's four of us, right? Our four girls. We're really close. We basically tell each other everything. We always have, you know?"

KJ nodded.

"So . . . after you told me about Matt's brother and stuff . . . I kind of told my other two friends. Not Katie, just the others. And, well, one of them, she's a good person but she does tend to network. I should have thought about that. I really shouldn't have told anybody, but we were all really worried about her. You know?"

KJ nodded again. "I know," he said.

"Do you?"

"Yeah."

"Well . . . so that's how it got out. My one friend told, I don't know, a few people, and that's how. I'm really sorry. Matt thinks Katie told. He broke up with her this morning."

KJ's head came up. "He did?"

"Yes. Have you talked to him?"

KJ shook his head.

"He was really rough on her, what he said," Tam told him. "She's very distraught. She's begging me to tell him what really happened, and I did try. But he wouldn't listen."

KJ nodded.

Tam said, "He was like, 'I don't want to hear this. It's all about me and my family.' "

"He doesn't mean to be that way," KJ said. "He's sort of in his own world right now."

"I wanted to smack him," she said.

KJ grinned. "Yeah?"

"Oh yeah."

"Well, you wouldn't be the first."

"So . . . you're okay? About this?"

He shrugged. "Hey, it had to come out. It was me who told you. Anyway, it's not your fault that it's happening in the first place."

"No."

"Or his," KJ said, and he studied her.

She nodded. "I know."

"It's tough for him. He doesn't know what to do. He's been trying to stay away, stay safe from it, *and* keep the lid on for such a long time. I don't think he knows what else to do."

"But he just lit into her. And then he dumped her for nothing. And she's my friend."

"I know. What are you gonna do?"

"We're looking for her. And for him," Tam said. "Katie said she was going to go find him. But we haven't seen her yet."

"Hmm. Or him?"

"No. Would he go home?"

"I don't think so," he said. "Not till later."

By now the buses had almost all left, and the stream of kids had dwindled to a few stragglers. Tam looked up the street:

Hope, standing by the last bus, gave a big shrug. Tam looked the other way, toward Grove Street. Samantha stood there all alone.

Tam stood up. "I'm going to her house," she said. "I think she's still there. Anyway, I hope so."

"Okay," KJ said, standing up, too. He was half a head shorter than her. "You still want to come out, after? To my place? To complete your defeat?"

"I . . . oh. Huh. I almost forgot about that."

"Well, I didn't," KJ said, and grinned.

"Let me see if I can work this stuff out first, okay? Then I'll come if I can. I want to. It's nine to five me, right?"

"It's eight to five you. Nice try. I'll be ready if you get there."

"You better not wear one of those Jordan shirts," Tam said. "I told you."

"We'll see about that."

"So where is your house?"

"Eighty-nine Grove Street," KJ said. "You just go straight out, that way. It's kind of a ways. If you run it, you'll be warmed up."

"Okay. I mean, I'll come if I can."

"Yeah. Cool. My house is right next to Matt's, by the way."

"It is?" she said. "Well, so . . . if you see her . . . or him . . . will you talk to them?"

"Yeah."

"Tell them what happened. Tell them it was me."

"I'll tell 'em it was us."

"Well . . . okay," she said. "Just don't let anybody do anything stupid."

He nodded once more. "I'll try."

"Cool." She took another breath. "Oh," she said. "Thanks."

"Don't forget—eighty-nine Grove," KJ said. "Number's on the mailbox. Come complete your defeat." And he went striding down School Street, past Sam, who studied him with a puzzled expression as he walked by.

DRIVEWAYS

When love rips a hole in you, sometimes you do crazy things. But was it so crazy and reckless for Katie to just want desperately to find him? To see him and talk to him and tell him the truth, even though she only knew one small part of the truth, that it hadn't been her?

Her mom had said that under no circumstances, none whatever, was Katie to leave this house before her mom got home. It was the only way that Darcy Henoch, who had had no choice but to go back to work, could try to keep her daughter safe today. When Darcy got home from the Price Chopper, she had told Katie, they could talk. But her mom was the last person Katie wanted to talk to. She knew Darcy would freak out, was no doubt already freaking out, silently saving it up as she stood at her register ringing up groceries—freaking inwardly about self-centered boys and terrible choices and consequences and so on and so on. Katie was too torn to pieces to hear it one more time.

Stabs of sharp feelings in her chest came and went, and after they went she would feel lost in a dark and bottomless emptiness. This was the real void, she was sure. All day she lay on her bed or roamed the apartment, tormented by the one hope she had—that if he just knew, if he only heard that part of the truth that she knew, this would all change. They would be back together and the world would be back the way it was meant to be: in one piece. Their one piece. She had known from the day she met him that this was how it was meant to be, that they were meant to be together—and now that their togetherness had been ripped apart, she felt torn away from herself.

She had to find him. She had to bring back what they had lost—because she was sure he was lost without her, too. He had to be. Thinking she had betrayed him? When she thought about him thinking this, she felt the stabbing and ripping in horrible ways, in physical ways that she could not stand. She could not stand this. It didn't matter what her mom said she was supposed to do or not do.

When school had let out and she knew he was out there somewhere, Katie left. She went out the back door so Mrs. Prescott, the older lady who lived downstairs and kept an eye out when Katie was home alone, might not notice. Katie opened the shed in back and got out her bike, partly so she could whiz by and be gone in case Mrs. Prescott did notice, but mainly because she wasn't sure where he would go, and she had to try to catch him. To cover ground. She had to.

Her bike, which she never rode anymore, was bright yellow. Her mom had picked that color years ago, so that her precious only daughter would be more visible to cars. And as Katie pulled it out she winced and wished, yet again, that it wasn't so horribly geeky. But she hopped on and swung quickly up the little driveway and past her building, going to Grove Street and away from school toward the place where she was hoping he would go. Maybe he would be there, waiting for her. Really maybe he would.

As she rode up to it, she first saw the big purple ice-cream cone in the window, but that was all she saw. He wasn't outside. She tried to look past the sign, through the window, to see if he might be inside. No sign of him. She pulled up to the store and leaned the bike against the brick wall. But inside she saw only the usual odd, sad people and stray kids from Jeffords. No him.

She felt desperate. Panicky. She hopped back on the bike and rode down State Street, retracing the steps they'd walked together past the gun store and the tanning parlor/laundromat, past the bars and the correctional center. Then up the steepening streets, past the houses. Breathing heavily now and working very hard, she churned up to stop at the end of the street, before the closed metal gate and the woods beyond.

She saw no one. She scrambled toward the little knob with the scar from the kids' bicycles. She rushed up to its top, where the almost-buried ancient rocks were, and the stunted pine trees. And nothing else.

Katie sat down and wanted to cry, but she was too scoured

now, and too desperate. She jumped back up, scrambled down the knob, and got back on her bike. Then she sat and thought, *Where? Where now?*

She could think of only one possible place. It was the one place where he would have to go eventually. She rode back down past the houses, and after she'd passed the correctional center she turned left, on the roads that ran behind Grove Street, parallel to it. She knew his house was out there, a ways out Grove Street among the nicer homes. The night after she'd met Matt, she had looked up his number. It was 91 Grove.

· · ● · ·

Mrs. Prescott was oddly tall for an older lady, almost as tall as Tam. In other ways she seemed normal: her gray hair was neatly pinned back, and the apartment behind her was full of lots of little things. Framed photos and many small treasures, porcelain and stuff like that. Tam could see no one else in there, except a big black cat who was sleeping on a flowered chair.

"Mrs. Prescott, have you seen Katie? I knocked upstairs but no one answered."

Mrs. Prescott's eyes widened. "She's supposed to be in there. She must be in there. Do you think she's sleeping?"

"I don't know. I knocked pretty loud."

Mrs. Prescott stepped out in the hall. She closed her door and glanced up the stairs.

"Let's go," she said, and she and Tam hurried up the stairs.

At Katie's door Mrs. Prescott rapped sharply, once and then again. They waited, listening. Mrs. Prescott put her ear to the door.

"I don't hear a single thing," she said.

"No," said Tam. "I didn't either."

"Oh, this is not a good thing. I was supposed to make sure she stayed."

Tam didn't answer.

"I suppose I ought to call her mother," Mrs. Prescott said, and winced. "She won't be one bit happy with me."

"Could you hold off for a little bit, and let me find her? I think I can find her," Tam said, though she wasn't at all sure.

"God, I hope so," Mrs. Prescott said. "Darcy was none too happy this morning. If I have to call her and she has to punch out early she'll be deranged. I'll be in as much trouble as poor Katie."

"Let me go find her. Okay?"

Mrs. Prescott nodded. "All right. Where did she go, do you think?"

"She's around. She's just looking for a friend."

"Oh well, thank goodness," Mrs. Prescott said. "How much trouble can she get into doing that? I mean, aren't we all just looking for a friend?"

She grinned lopsidedly at Tam, who, to be polite, returned the smile. "I guess so," she said. "Thanks."

But as she trotted out the front door, Tam had no idea which way to go. Where did Katie and Matt go together? Tam had no clue. She started down the sidewalk, looking and think-

215

ing, then stopped and turned. Down Katie's little driveway, the door of the backyard shed was open. Tam walked over and looked in. Katie's bright yellow bike was gone.

Oh crap, Tam thought. *There's no way to catch her now.*

Tam could think of only one thing. If she went out to KJ's house, to finish beating him—he'd said the house was next to Matt's. Could they see his driveway from KJ's? Matt's house would be the one place Katie might go, or might end up going if she couldn't find him anywhere else. Right?

Right, she thought. She went trotting up Grove Street, then broke into a run.

·· ● ··

The number "91" was on a tree, next to the driveway. Katie turned in, stopping just beyond the tree, and peered. A long driveway sloped upward. She couldn't see much from here.

She walked cautiously up the drive. There was a broad lawn and a big white house, with the driveway circling in front of it. Then she saw that the driveway split, so that it also went back behind the house. Across the lawn to the right was another house, this one cream-colored, with dark red shutters and a basketball hoop above the garage. She saw no one there or anywhere.

School had been out for almost an hour. If Matt had come right home, he would be here by now. It was her only chance, though she wondered vaguely whether it would be trespassing to wait around outside if he wasn't here.

She didn't want to go knock on that big front door. It looked too formal, like the real people and the kids would go around back. Nervously, tentatively, she walked her bike up the driveway, alert for any sounds of barking or rushing dogs but not hearing anything at all.

Katie followed the asphalt around the side of the house. Here in back was a two-car garage, with both doors closed. The driveway spread out wide, like a dark pool, in front of the garage. No cars were out here. Also in back of the house was a big patio, with what looked like a set of kitchen windows looking out on it. Katie, venturing closer, could see a kitchen in there. Farther along was a regular-looking door. As she came slowly up to it, she heard music from inside. It was harsh-sounding music, thrash or metal. Matt had said he mostly liked hip-hop. This wasn't that, but it was definitely not a grownup's music.

She leaned her bike against the side of the house, by the door with the music behind it. Beside the door was a double window, but inside curtains were drawn across. She couldn't see anything. She took a deep, deep breath, and another. Then she stepped to the door and knocked.

MOVES

About ten minutes later, when Tam came up KJ's driveway, she saw that you could keep an eye on Matt's house from here. KJ's house was cream-colored, with dark red shutters, and Tam liked it. Matt's was plain white, big but uninteresting, like it was a fancy house bought from a catalog. Tam saw how Matt's driveway curved around back, behind the garage that stuck out backward so you couldn't see where the driveway ended, back in there. But you could see the front door, and you could definitely also see if anyone came in or out from the back. Tam decided this was good. This was the best place she could be.

KJ was just coming outside, a basketball under his arm. He was wearing a light blue Washington Wizards jersey. Number 23. The last one Jordan wore.

"Hey," Tam said. "Thought I told you not to wear one of those."

KJ smiled. "Exactly why I wore it." He turned, squared up,

rose about an inch off the asphalt, and shot. The ball went in. He turned back and looked her up and down.

"What'd you do, run the whole way? You're all sweaty."

"I'm warmed up, is what," she said. "And you better get loose."

He nodded, turned, and shot again. Tam said to his back, "You didn't see her, did you?"

"No."

"Did you look?"

"Well, I wasn't *watching*. Was I supposed to?"

"No, no. It's all right. I just want to make sure I keep an eye out. For either of them."

"They might have got together by now," KJ said. "It's possible."

Tam nodded. Well, there wasn't anything she could do about it at this moment. When a rebound bounced off, she strode in and grabbed it.

"Tell me when you're ready," she said, turning to shoot.

"Hey," KJ said, "I am ready."

· · ● · ·

When he opened the door, Katie knew this was Matt's brother. He was tall and skinny; his All-Star Basketball Camp T-shirt hung loosely from wire-hanger shoulders. The music was jagged behind him. He looked her up and down. Then, without asking who she was or what she wanted or anything, which seemed odd to her, he turned and walked back inside the shade-darkened room. He left the door open for her. She followed, closing the door behind her and thinking, Well, maybe he knew who she was. Maybe he was leading her to his brother or something.

Neal's room had a pale leather couch facing a TV that wasn't on. Beside the couch was a chair, also pale leather, and behind the couch a bed, which was a mess. There were messes all around, in piles. There was a table between the couch and TV, and Neal sat down on the couch. He nodded at the chair next to him, and she went over and sat there. Then she realized she was in *his* house, in Matt's house, where he had said it wasn't cool for her to come. She knew that if he saw her here, he'd be even more furious. He'd be *so* mad at her. A spasm of fear and hopelessness shrank her up inside.

"What are you," Neal said. "Fourteen?"

"Fifteen."

"This your first time, or what?"

"Um . . . what?"

"You know." He slid over, so he was closer.

"I . . . I was looking for Matt."

"For what?"

"For Matt. Aren't you Neal?"

"Oh. Yeah. Matt. Uh . . . I don't think he's around."

Katie sank deeper into the soft chair. She'd had nobody to be with and talk to, all day long. She asked him, "Does he ever talk about me? Katie?"

"Uh . . . not that I know of," Neal said. "But whatever."

Now she shrank into nothing. Her face crinkled up and she couldn't help crying.

"I don't know what to do," she said, covering her face, ashamed to be like this. "It's just so *awful*. I don't know what happened." She was shaking her head, hiding her face, crying as she had been crying all day. "It feels so bad," she said.

Neal got up, went over and put on some smooth, pulsating music. Katie didn't know it, but it was kind of like Prince. Neal came back and sat down close.

"It doesn't have to," he said softly.

Her face came up, all wet.

"It doesn't?"

"No."

"Can you do something?"

"Oh yeah."

He went over by his bed and brought back a box of tissues. He put it on the table before her, then sat down again and reached under his couch. He drew out a tray and set it on the table. It had some different things on it—a box of Q-tips, a cell phone, two spoons, and some tiny, zip-closed plastic bags. Katie was blurry in her misery and didn't look closely, but she remembered now, in a vague way, what it was she was supposed to have told. About Neal. That he was dealing.

She wiped her eyes and watched. She felt a pulsation along with the music. Neal pulled open one of the tiny bags. He tapped some soft-looking, light-colored powder out onto a spoon, then carefully zipped the bag closed again. He held up the spoon, close to Katie's nose.

"Go ahead," he said. "Sniff it up. You won't feel bad anymore."

Up close, the powder looked just like iced-tea mix. Katie and her mom used to make iced tea from mix like that, together, when Katie was younger and they did things together. Katie felt a new jab of pain, knowing how hard she'd been on her mom and how mad her mom was going to be when she came home and Katie wasn't there. And how mad Matt was. Everybody she loved was mad at her. She didn't know why. It was horrible. The powder didn't look horrible. It looked like iced-tea mix. He said she wouldn't feel bad anymore.

"Sniff it up," Neal said. "It's easy."

It was.

GAME POINT

Tam scored first. She drove on KJ, scrambling to her right; she lifted up a wild, floating scoop shot that never should have gone in, but did. It was winner's outs, so he took the ball as it fell through and bounce-passed it back.

"You can't tell me you practiced that," he said.

Tam said nothing, just dribbled. As she did she glanced at the side of Matt's house. No sign. While she was looking, KJ lunged; he tapped the ball loose and kept going to grab it. Tam wanted to say *Hey, no fair, I was looking for them.* But she didn't. She just dug in.

"What are we playing to?" she said. "Fifteen?"

"Sure."

"Okay."

KJ's steal and all the day's tensions now energized her. She was up on him, her arms wide and flailing, snatching at the ball, complicating his moves. He tried turning and backing her in, but her arms were everywhere. Finally she rushed him into taking a fallaway shot, the kind Matt had said never to do anymore. KJ heard that message in his head—*Bad choice! No control!*—and sure enough the ball hit nothing as it fell way short. Tam seized it while he was still stumbling backward.

· ● · ·

It was all gone, all the pain and anguish, the desperation and the fear . . . all evaporated. Katie didn't feel bad, she didn't feel good. She didn't feel anything. She was just floating, completely uncaring, not caring at all about anything. It was like that time she'd had her tonsils out, when she was almost eleven; right before they took her into the operating room they gave her something so she wasn't scared at all anymore. It was warm and floaty, that time. She hadn't minded that they were wheeling her in to cut something out of her, she hadn't cared at all. This was like that.

She didn't care that Neal was taking her hand and drawing her over to the couch with him. She didn't care at all that he kept hold of her hand, and now that he was moving his hand up and down her arm, not saying anything at all, and the music was smooth. She was smooth and she didn't care that he had his hands on her now. She did maybe care a little about that; there was a small voice inside her saying, "Not this . . . not this," but she wasn't listening to it. She didn't care.

Now his hands were on her breasts outside her shirt and the little far-back voice was saying, "Not this, not this," and now he was opening her shirt, undoing the buttons, and Katie said vaguely, "Um . . . don't. Don't."

"It's cool," he said, and kept on.

"No. Please." She didn't care that much, but part of her did. "Please don't," she said again and pushed his hands down, away.

"Hey, listen, I gave you half a bag, all right? So relax. Enjoy it."

He put his hands back on her breasts and Katie shook her head. "No," she said. "No," and pushed them away again.

"Oh yeah?" he said. "Fucking *bitch*!" And he rose up and smacked her hard across the face with the back of his hand.

Katie fell back. This was too much. She didn't feel any hurt from the blow, no pain at all, just overload. This was too much. It was all too much, and it was easier just to fall back, to let herself fall back and not care, just not be here. She could let herself go in it. Just check out.

And she was out. Neal drew back and looked at her. He cursed softly. Then he shrugged. He went to make himself a small hit, before going on with it. He took his time.

· · ● · ·

KJ couldn't do much. She had his game boxed in, and she was playing wild—keeping him rushed and flustered when he had the ball, then zooming all over with the dribble when she had it. Some of her off-balance shots were way off, but some went in.

He'd scored a few times but now it was fourteen to nine, game point and Tam had the ball yet again. She was starting to dribble when KJ spotted Matt walking up the driveway toward them.

Coming up to KJ's, Matt saw them and stopped. He'd grown tired of walking and listening to tunes and thought he would come shoot with KJ. He could hang out with KJ, and he wanted to hang out with somebody. He really wanted to. So he was shocked and irritated when he saw the tall girl from French class, the annoying one who had already made a very bad day even worse. What was *she* doing here?

The annoying girl was dribbling, her back to Matt. He saw KJ take her elbow and say something, and she spun around. She saw him and now, *damn*, she was running down the driveway. KJ came chugging behind.

"Where is she?" the girl called as she came up. "Have you seen her?"

Matt didn't answer. No way did he want to deal with this. But now KJ came up, all sweaty and out of breath. He bent over, heaving, and looked up at Matt.

"Come on, man," he gasped out. "This is important."

The annoying girl stepped up too close. "She's been looking for you since school let out," she said. "She's on a yellow bike. You've seen her, right?"

"No. I don't want to, either."

The girl grabbed his shirt. "Listen, dork, you broke her into little tiny pieces for no reason, all right? It wasn't her who told. She had nothing to do with it. It was us."

"What?" Matt looked at KJ. KJ's face was pained.

"He told me what's going on 'cause he's worried about you, all right?" the girl said. "I didn't mean to let it out to everyone— I just told my two other best friends, last night, and one of them let it out. It just happened, and Katie had nothing to do with it—but then *you* figure she did it and you slice her up and dump her like trash and now she's out there in a million pieces, looking for you. God knows *why*," the girl said, and pushed him away.

Matt was stunned. He looked at KJ, who said, "Go call her, man. Call her. Maybe she's home."

Matt nodded, turned, and sprinted for his house. He came around the garage and in the back he saw a bright yellow bicycle, leaning against the wall beside Neal's door.

He threw open the door and there was Neal, on top of her—and as he came closer it didn't look like Katie was moving. Neal's hands were inside her shirt; he rose and turned as Matt drove right through him, lifted him off the floor and smashed him against the wall. Neal's head thunked back hard against the wall and he fell to the floor.

Matt bent to Katie and cupped her head. "Katie! Katie, *wake up*! Oh Jesus, *wake up*!" She didn't respond. Matt stood up trying to think what to do when Neal, coming up from the floor, knocked him hard off his feet and he sprawled over the table and fell backward to the floor.

"Get out," Neal said. "She's fine."

"She doesn't wake up!"

"She's *fine*."

"How much did she take, Neal?"

"She's *fine*. She just nodded. Now get out before I hurt you."

Matt put his hands on the floor to push himself up and felt something hard. He looked; it was Neal's cell phone.

Matt had Carolyn Casey's card in his wallet, but he didn't want her, he wanted an ambulance. He flipped the phone open and dialed 911.

"Hey!" Neal said. "Are you *crazy*?"

Neal lunged for the phone, grabbing at it, but Matt had his feet under him now and he sprang forward, catching Neal's chest with his shoulder and driving him back. Neal fell over the table and tumbled backward onto the floor. Matt lifted the table's front edge with his free hand and flipped it on top of Neal. He sat down hard on the underside of the table, holding all his weight down on it with Neal underneath. He lifted the phone to his ear just as the emergency operator came on.

Matt gave his address and said there was a girl here who needed help. Neal was squirming and cursing under the table, shoving at it. The table rolled and bucked under Matt like a raft in a hurricane.

"Come fast!" Matt shouted at the phone. "She took drugs. She might have OD'd. It's bad!"

"Is she conscious?"

"No!"

"All right. Is she breathing?"

Matt looked over, saw her chest rise and fall. "Yeah."

"All right. How old is she?"

"Uh . . . fifteen."

"Okay. Stay with her. Don't leave her, all right?"

"Okay." Beneath him Neal squirmed loose and the table slapped hard to the floor. The movement rolled Matt to his back, and Neal snatched the cell phone. As he grabbed it the phone snapped shut, hanging itself up. Matt sprang to his feet as Neal opened the phone again, held it to his ear, then turned the phone off.

"You fucking *idiot*," he said. "What did you *do*?"

Matt was bent now in the defensive stance, his hands open and ready. Neal's paraphernalia were all over the floor. Matt looked over; Katie was still out. Neal glanced at her, too.

"You moron, she just nodded—that's all," he said. "You don't know *anything*. Ah, God, what did you *do*?"

Neal fell to his knees and scrabbled around on the floor, grabbing at stuff. He reached under the couch, at Matt's feet, his hands groping around. He was pulling things out and stuffing them in his pockets. Matt bent over, latched on to Neal, and rolled him away on the floor; his brother gathered himself and sprang at Matt, who lost his balance and fell. Matt came back at him and they wrestled around for a few seconds. Neal kept trying to shove Matt out of the way so he could get at his stuff, while Matt grappled to control his brother, to keep him down and wrap him up. Then they both heard a siren in the distance. Neal tore himself away, panic and fear in his eyes. He snatched a couple more things off the floor, then sprang toward the door and half ran, half stumbled through it.

Matt went to the door. Neal was running into the woods

beyond the house. Matt watched him, then went back inside.

Katie was shaking her head. She said, "What . . . ooh. *Ow.*" She opened her eyes. "Matt?"

· · ● · ·

Carolyn Casey's work space at the city police headquarters had one window, a desk piled with papers and files, a small table, and a set of shelves. Little framed photos were lined up on the table and across the shelves, in front of various binders and manuals and reference books. The photos were of her family and friends, various Casey relatives who lived in and around Rutland—babies, kids at birthday parties, high school graduates in caps and gowns, wedding couples, kids in football and soft-ball and basketball uniforms. There were also models and photos of the vintage American motorcycles that were the young detective's other great interest. One of her dreams was someday to own a classic Indian or an old Harley. She was gazing absently at the photos when the emergency dispatcher's voice crackled out from the scanner on the table.

"Central to regional ambulance. Would you respond, Code Two, to 91 Grove Street in Rutland, for possible overdose. Caller advises fifteen-year-old female is unconscious but breathing. No other information is available, the 911 call from a young male was interrupted. Called back, no answer."

Carolyn Casey knew the address. She was out the office door and down the stairs before the dispatcher had signed off.

······●······

When you hear a siren in the distance, one part of your brain stays with it, tracking the sound as you go on with whatever you were doing. If the siren comes steadily closer, more and more of your attention goes toward it. After Matt had run to his home, KJ and Tam had stood unsurely, awkwardly, in KJ's driveway. Neither wanted to start playing again, even though it had been game point. Even Tam wasn't thinking about the game. They were standing around hoping Matt would reappear. It was taking a little while; they both wondered if that meant he was talking to her on the phone.

As the siren came closer they looked at each other. When it was clearly approaching fast on Grove Street, they both turned toward the road. The sound came very close and did not go by. When the green-and-white boxy ambulance started up Matt's driveway, its red lights whirling, both Tam and KJ broke for Matt's house. They went running together across the lawns.

······●······

Matt was standing waiting before the front door of his house. The ambulance came up the long driveway and stopped, its square body lurching once on the wheels. The two front doors swung open and two people in bright white shirts and dark pants leaped out.

"Where is she?" said the first one, a guy. The other, the driver, was a woman, short and dark-haired. They were both kind of young. The man had a sort of toolbox. They came right up on the front steps, wanting to go in.

"It's okay," Matt said. "It's okay."

"What? Where is she?" the guy said again. "Take us to her."

"No, really, it's okay," Matt said. "I made a mistake. She was just sleeping. I came home and I thought something was wrong, but it wasn't. Everything's fine. Really."

The short woman studied him skeptically. "Show us," she said. "Take us to her." She moved to go in the house.

Matt sidestepped to block her, holding up his hands. "Really," he said. "Really, okay? It's okay. She's fine. She doesn't need anything. She really . . ."

All three of them turned as another siren started up the driveway. It came from a plain blue sedan that snaked up fast and then braked hard behind the ambulance. Matt saw a woman's reddish-blond head pop up from the driver's opening door. His own head felt like it was coming loose.

· • ● • ·

KJ and Tam had run to the front of the house and now they stood there, watching Matt seem to be trying to stop the two rescue squad people from going in the big front door when the plain blue car came howling up the driveway and stopped behind the ambulance. They saw Matt sort of sag backward as a young woman with strawberry-blond hair hopped out and hustled up to the group on the steps. KJ and Tam came closer, to hear.

"Matt," Carolyn Casey said. "Who is it? Where is she?"

"He's saying she's all right," the dark-haired woman from the ambulance said. "He's saying she was just, what, napping?" She looked at Matt and he nodded nervously.

"All right," Detective Casey said. "Matt, who's home?"

"Nobody."

"Where's your brother?"

"He's not here."

"Mom? Dad?"

"Working."

"Who's inside? Who is the girl, Matt?"

"A friend."

"Of Neal's? Of yours?"

"Mine."

"Was she using?"

For a second Matt didn't answer.

"Matt, we need to see this girl. We need to see her right now."

Matt's jaw dropped, but no words had yet come out when the front door opened behind him, just opened a few inches and stopped.

Everybody on the steps turned toward the door. A voice from behind the door, loud and firm enough for Tam and KJ to hear, said, "Matt. Tell them."

Matt was speechless. Katie stepped out through the open

door. She looked shaky and pale but she stepped up to Matt, looking only at him.

"Tell them," she said.

Matt took a step back and put his hands on her shoulders. "Please," he said to her. "Go back inside, okay? It'll be . . ."

"*Tell* them." Katie folded her arms and stared into his eyes. Matt's hands fell.

"Tell them," she said again. "Right here. If you don't, I will."

Matt took a breath and let it out. He turned to Detective Casey.

"All right," he said.

"Let's go inside," Carolyn Casey said. As they went through the door, she motioned for the rescue crew to come, too. KJ and Tam were left out on the lawn, watching as the front door closed.

INTERVIEW ROOM

She's *not* a druggie," Matt told Detective Casey a while later, in an interview room upstairs at the police station. It was a small room, with one window and a table at which they sat, facing each other. The door to the big room where all the detectives worked was open.

"I can't believe she would do that," he said. "Maybe Neal fooled her or something."

"I doubt it," Carolyn Casey said. She spoke carefully. "The world isn't divided into people who would use hard drugs and those who would never, Matt. From my experience it's much more that someone, it could be anyone really, is in the wrong place at the wrong time, when they're very upset or under a whole lot of stress. When they're really vulnerable, and the opportunity is there. That's when it happens. Don't think this was so unusual."

Matt put his head in his hands. "It was my fault. It totally was. I wouldn't listen to her."

Detective Casey studied him. "Don't beat yourself up too bad. If you hadn't come after her, she might still be in there."

Matt groaned. "God."

"As it is, she should be all right. They're keeping her overnight at the hospital, for observation. But they say she seems okay. She's pretty sore, all over. Not just where he hit her. This drug leaves you that way."

Matt couldn't look at her. "What a mess," he said. "What a total mess."

"Listen. Matt. I know you were trying to protect your brother. I understand that. I'm not sure you understood what was at stake, really."

"I did," he said. "I think I did. I just didn't know what to do."

"Yeah. I get that."

"What'll happen to Neal?" It was the question Matt had been most scared to ask.

"When we found him, he had ditched whatever he may have had on him," she said. "We haven't found that, though we're still looking. But we found enough heroin in his room to charge possession with intent to distribute. It's his first offense, and he's well known in the community, but he was clearly dealing, in a small-time way. It'll be up to the state's attorney to decide what charges to bring. Usually the courts favor a commitment to rehab in a situation like this. He may face some jail time as well. It's hard to say at this point."

She saw the emotion in Matt's eyes. She understood. She was a family person, too.

"Matt. Understand. This is probably the best thing that could have happened for your brother. First of all, he's alive. Second, this stops the process, at least for now. He'll be ordered into treatment and rehab, whether he goes to jail or not. If he wants to get clean and if he really works the recovery program, he has a chance. He has a shot. He can be your brother again. But I'm not going to lie to you. This is a long, hard road. It just is. He'll need your help, and your family's, but whether he can make it is really going to be up to him. Some people do. A lot don't. This drug just keeps dragging them back, and in the end it swallows up their lives."

Matt was looking at the floor.

"Jeez, I was going to try to make you feel better," Carolyn Casey said. "Guess I screwed *that* up." She laughed, in a small way. Matt smiled in a small way, still looking at the floor.

"This is not the end of the story, Matt," she said, carefully again. "But your brother is alive, and things are in the open now. That may cause some turbulence, but you and I both know it's better than how it was."

Matt nodded. That word "turbulence" reminded him of something. "Are my parents here? Did you talk to them?"

"Of course they are, and sure I did. They're downstairs."

"How are they?"

She smiled. "Well, I would say they're stunned. And obviously upset."

"They're going to kill me."

"I don't think so. But I wouldn't want to be in your brother's position right about now."

Matt looked up at her. "When you first talked to me, that time by the school . . . did you really think it was me?"

Carolyn shrugged. "My job's not to jump to conclusions. There were some red flags in your behavior. But once I'd talked to you, I just didn't have the feeling you were into something really serious. I wasn't sure, but it seemed more like you were . . . protecting somebody."

Matt gave another small smile. "I never called you."

"Nope. And you didn't want to let us in the house," she reminded him. "You're a pretty headstrong guy, that's my impression. I think you're lucky that girl finally stood up to you."

Matt nodded thoughtfully. Now he looked into Carolyn Casey's eyes. "You're a, you know—a girl and stuff."

She laughed. "It's shocking, but true."

"I mean, no offense."

"None taken."

"But, I mean . . . you think she'll, you know . . ."

"Take you back? Ever speak to you again?"

"Well . . . yeah." They had taken Katie off in the ambulance. Standing there with his friends, looking at her, Matt couldn't tell what she was thinking. After they had insisted on loading her onto that stretcher and lifting her into the back of the vehicle, she had seemed so far away, and she had given him such a faraway look. After the ambulance left, as it all came together in his mind—as he saw how he had acted and what he had allowed to happen—he thought maybe she would never, ever trust him again. He wouldn't blame her if she didn't.

Carolyn Casey thought for a second. "Hard to say," she said. "Her mom may not be real big on you right now. As for the girl . . . how much do you like her?"

Matt looked down again. "A lot."

"A whole lot?"

"Yeah."

"A whole no-matter-what-happens lot?"

Matt smiled. "I think so."

"Hmm." She nodded. "Is . . . this the first time? That you've felt that way?"

"Well, yeah. Basically. Before I wrecked it."

She smiled. "You might get another chance."

"You think?"

Carolyn shrugged. "Hey, it's up to the girl. But you can try."

"How do you do it?" he asked. "I mean, how do you do it right?"

"Beats me," she said. "Basically it beats everybody. I think you just . . . try. And, with luck, you learn."

"Huh."

"Of course, you might start by not withholding any big hairy awful secrets the next time around."

He shook his head. "That doesn't work, huh?"

"It tends not to."

"Yeah."

She gazed at him. The kid was growing up before her eyes, she thought. It was like looking at time-lapse photography.

"If you want to get close to someone, you might as well be straight with them," she said. "A reasonably conscious woman will usually figure you out sooner or later anyway."

"Really? Girls are kind of like detectives, huh?"

"Pretty much. Sometimes they *are* detectives."

"Huh. But, so . . . what should I do now?"

"You mean with her?"

"Yeah."

"Well, I would say . . . be patient. Apologize. Explain yourself. Apologize again. Be totally honest and real. Then you might need to let some time pass. But in my limited experience, when two people really care for each other, that can bring them through a whole lot of stuff. But trust, you know—that can take a while to rebuild. Just be patient. Be real. And show her. Keep finding ways to show her."

Slowly Matt nodded. He was looking at the table.

"Well, hey," Carolyn Casey said. "Guess that's not the kind of advice you'd expect from a detective, huh?"

Matt didn't answer. He seemed lost in thought.

"On another subject," she said. "Think you'll play ball again? For Rutland?"

Matt looked up. "Huh? Oh." He shrugged. "Guess I could, huh?"

"Guess you could."

"Well . . . maybe I will."

Detective Casey shook her head. "It pains me, as a loyal graduate of Mount St. Joseph Academy, to think I may have done anything, however indirectly, to benefit a Rutland High School sports program."

"Hey, don't beat yourself up," Matt said, smiling again. "You were just doing your job."

"That I was. And in the dark days to come, when you're torching us for twenty-five or thirty points a game, I will try to keep telling myself that."

"Okay."

"I'll be there," she said, more seriously. "I'll be watching."

"Oh jeez. I better keep my nose clean, huh?"

"You goddamn well better, young man. You have too much to live for."

He nodded. "I know."

She stood up. "Matt, it's been a long evening. Your parents need to get you home." She stuck out her hand. He stood up and shook it.

"Remember what happened today," she said, looking into his eyes. "Remember it. Nobody died. Believe me, it doesn't always work out that way."

Matt nodded. "Thanks," he said, and he meant it. He turned to go. Carolyn Casey watched him walk out the door, and go back to his life. As he went she whispered a small prayer of thanks.

ACKNOWLEDGMENTS

Rutland, Vermont, is not only a real place, it's the place where I live. All the characters in this novel are completely fictional, as is Jeffords Junior High School and the homes described on and off Grove Street, along with their house numbers, though the street itself is actual. Yet this little city's passion for youth sports, and the caring and support that many adults offer to young people here, are very real. So are the urgent dangers to teenagers that this story depicts—dangers that are ever-present today in cities and towns of all types and sizes.

I am very grateful to Detective Sergeant Kevin Stevens of the Rutland City Police Department, for his time and expert advice; and to Hannah Schoenberg, Aviva Markowitz, and Sarah Seigle, the original "brain trust," along with Emma Schoenberg. Thanks also to Desirée Clark, a courageous young woman whose honest guidance was indispensable to the making of this book; to Zach Krasner for the IM expertise; to Gail Hochman, my agent, who knows her stuff and really cares; and to Wesley Adams, my wise and insightful editor at Farrar, Straus and Giroux.

In many ways, *Falling* grew out of my involvement with students and staff at the Rutland Middle School, where for several recent years I helped to lead a weekly after-school writers' group. I am grateful to all the members of the Pen Works Young Writers Project at R.M.S., and to Jennifer Enzor, the language-arts teacher with whom I worked on the project. I am also indebted to school counselor Tom Chamberlain, to Laura Foley, an R.M.S. teacher, and to the eighth-grade classes that helped me develop the main characters in this novel in spring 2003. Thanks to each of those students—and to the group of excellent eighth-grade readers at Rutland Middle who, in spring 2004, spent a number of their lunch periods with me, reading and critiquing early drafts of the opening chapters of this book. One of the best pieces of encouragement I've ever received came when one young woman scribbled in the margin of a page, "This is way true."

I hope so. Thanks, in the end, to everyone who helped.

D.W.
Rutland, Vermont